A
Spacious Place

*"You have not given me into
the hands of the enemy but have
set my feet in a spacious place."*

Psalm 31:8

L. KEPHART-NASH

outskirts
press

Curt Swarm, Writer, Metal Sculptor, Photographer, Creative Writing Teacher and Author of the "Empty Nest" Newspaper Column

"L. Kephart-Nash's second book, 'A Spacious Place' is a well-written, sensitive, murder-mystery that has as its central theme female abuse: physical, mental and emotional. It's an intriguing tale of chase, catch, escape, repeat. Nash keeps the reader turning pages to find out what's in store for the heroine, villain and supporting cast of "rescuers." As in her first book, "When the Tempest Passes and the Wicked is no More," Nash's prose is first rate, poetic and charming. All perpetrators get their just due, as Nash weaves a wicked, intricate tale of revenge, paybacks, and sleight-of-hand discoveries. What do you do to someone who has harmed you or someone dear to you? Well, you.......read how Nash deals with her persona non grata.

I look forward to L. Kephart-Nash's third book."

ILLUSTRATOR
DANIEL W. HATALA, BIO

A native Iowan, Dan has spent his entire working career as an artist. After studying commercial art, Dan started his career as an Art Director at Midwest agency. He became Senior Illustrator at a well-known art studio that allowed him to work with many nationally known companies. Dan's niche as a technical illustrator has enabled him to work for clients such as Danbury Mint, Masterpieces Puzzles, Budweiser, Coors, Pizza Hut, AMC Theaters, Ducks Unlimited, Sears and many others. In 1996, Dan began working on his own as a freelance artist and has enjoyed working from his home studio for the past 20 years. In the late 1990's Dan became an illustrator for the United States Air Force and has had the privilege of traveling to many bases around the world.

In Dan's free time, he enjoys motorcycles, hunting, fishing, and the outdoors.

Dan continues to live and work from his home studio in Waverly, Iowa.

Note: Dan's work became known to L. Kephart-Nash through the illustrations he created for her adult grandsons' children's book, "Like My Dad Always Said" which debuted in 2018 for Father's Day.

A SPACIOUS PLACE
LIST OF CHARACTERS

DES MOINES	Martha (Marti) Gracek-Sweltzer	Subject of In A Spacious Place
	Scotty & Nancy Gracek	Marti's parents
	Julia Gracek	Marti's sister
	Harold & Nancy Bolin	Marti's stepfather
	Shirley & Ben Hebner	Hairdresser & husband
	Theodore "Ted" Sweltzer	Marti's husband
	Josey & Wencel Sweltzer	Ted's parents
	Peggy & Donna	Ted's sisters
	Rachel	Minister's young wife
	Audra O'Neil	Wealthy socialite
	Lonnie & Mort	Two inept crooks
	Archie Reid	Dishonest policeman
	Tate Osborn	Police detective
	Joe	Police officer
DECORAH	Thora & Gilbert Iverson	Landlords
	Emma & Nels Rasmusson	1st clients of Marti
	Curtis & Roxann Truman	2nd clients of Marti
	Sena Dahl	3rd client of Marti
	Chris Losinski	Ex G.I. / carpenter
	Gulliver	Stray dog
RED WING	Fay Hessel & Gordon	Landlady and grandson
	Mincemeat	Stray cat
	Lucy Radstone & Fern	Neighbor, Lucy's housekeeper
	Rolo Smith	Homeless man
	Martin	Owner of Martin's Food Stand
	Kathy & J.D. Webb	Policewoman & attorney husband
	Mitch	Police Officer
	Delano (Del) Robertson	Acquaintance from past
	Gaye, Neal & Jack	Del's ex, Del's sons

TABLE OF CONTENTS

INTRODUCTION

"Please do not annoy the writer, she may put you in a book and kill you." That message was emblazoned on a cup, a gift from a daughter whose wild and wonderful sense of humor always made her mother laugh. Tamara sent it when she'd heard her mother had finished writing what she called her "first, last, and only" book just days before her 83rd birthday.

Holding the cup, gazing into the cherry red interior, rereading the clever message in black letters on white background, the elderly woman laughed softly again, delighted with her daughter's teasing.

Then without bothering to wash, or even rinse the new cup, she set it on the Keurig, inserted a K-cup—Nantucket, her favorite flavor—and brewed herself that wonderful first hot cup of coffee of the day. And in contentment sat at her table, gazing out on a lovely, sunny morning filled with the sound of songbirds. With each lift of the cup to her mouth, the message in large black letters began to resonate somewhere deep in the recesses of her memory. Was it really fifty years since she'd heard that cry in the dead of night? The thoughts floating back gave her pause. The quiet aloneness invited introspection. Minutes slipped by unnoticed, the woman immobile. There was something that needed exposure, and holding the cup with a message, a tale began arranging itself—quietly, steadily, inexorably in the old woman's mind. And yes, she certainly knew individuals deserving of being put in a book and killed.

Smiling into her cup, she sang "Happy Birthday" to herself, and then went down to her basement work room and scribbled a layout for "A SPACIOUS PLACE." It was May 11th—2020.

1960'S-70'S MARTHA

To some, the silence pervading the spacious but bland rooms of the house might have seemed oppressive, but for the lone figure listlessly tidying what was already tidy, and wiping what was already spotless, the silence was precious. The woman wanted to be alone, left in peace, but already was dreading the moment when the sound of the car would be heard on the drive, the slam of the car door—and inevitably the kitchen door would open. And only God knew what mood he would be in! The time was closer, and she knew it, to when she would have to leave to survive.

She walked soundlessly in stocking feet, a duster in one hand, the other tugging up the loose-fitting slacks as they sagged downwards. They needed taking in, as did most of the things in her closet. Ted watched what she ate, "for her own good," he said. Not that she had ever been fat. He simply couldn't abide overweight people and was making sure she did not become one. He, himself, worked out regularly at a gym, and was an avid golfer with his business associates. He still looked much as he did when she'd first met him and had been awestruck, thinking him the most beautiful man she'd ever seen. Tall, with wavy blond hair, blue-eyed, tanned, Ted could have passed for a movie star. She could hardly believe it when he had shown interest in her. He came from a well-to-do family. And with his stunning good looks could have had his pick of any girl, but he had picked her! Her! She had found work in a bank in Des Moines after graduation and left home. Their paths had crossed there, and she had been over the moon in love with him. At nineteen she married him. Everything had seemed so perfect at first. She couldn't pinpoint exactly when things began changing, but now, sixteen years later, though Ted looked much the same, he repulsed her, filled her with fear and dread. She needed—had to get away from him and had begun thinking through what she could do to prepare a way out. He'd said he'd kill her if she tried to leave. He'd been drinking when he said it, but she believed him. The physical violence was worse and more often. And recovery took longer. It could not continue.

To learn several years into the marriage that Ted did not like or want children had been a bitter disappointment. One of the first of many disillusionments of life with Ted. At least it made leaving him easier as she considered ways to escape.

As she moved from cupboard to dining room, from stove to sink, from refrigerator to drawer, Martha wondered if she looked like a puppet, its strings being pulled, putting her through all the scripted moves. Ted expected his dinner to be ready when he arrived home from his office in his father's insurance/real estate business. Tonight, he wanted a roast with fresh peas and carrots, and roasted early golden potatoes. A fresh spinach salad was in the refrigerator along with a homemade lemon meringue pie. Rolls would be warmed last minute. The dining room table was set with place settings at the head and foot of its polished surface. His port wine ready and waiting. A crystal candle holder held three white candles. The china was a wedding gift from Ted's parents, Josey and Wencel. The silver had been passed down from Josey's deceased parents. Silverware that Wencel had brought out and given the young couple ten years earlier. Martha had noted at the time the shock on Josey's face, and realized her mother-in-law had been unaware the gift was to be made. Also noted was how fast the woman's face became expressionless. Martha now knew a great deal more about the well-to-do Sweltzers. And the two silent sisters, Peggy and Donna, who, behind their backs, Ted called "Piggy" and "Dummy." Both had married right out of high school and were now living out of state.

Casually pushing the spinach around her plate, eating minute bits slowly, and chewing everything thoroughly, Martha timed the consumption of the salad to the time it took Ted to complete his dinner. When he leaned back in his chair lifting his second glass of wine, and sipping, Martha rose and quietly removed the plates and silver, returning to the kitchen to dish up the lemon meringue pie. She performed all these actions without a sound. Ted did not like clatter. With a dessert plate in each hand, Martha placed a generous slice of pie in front of Ted, and a sliver of a piece at her own place at the foot of the table. And didn't miss her husband's reaction. The glitter in his eyes, the stillness of his posture followed by the soft, cold expressionless voice. "You don't need that." And carefully she pushed the plate with the sliver of pie to the side, and turning her attention to her water glass, murmured, "Of course— you're right." But she knew what was coming, and she felt as though she were freezing; as though she couldn't breathe deep enough, her heart fluttering in her chest.

"Do something with your hair. You're a mess!"

"Yes. Yes—I will! I'll call Shirley first thing tomorrow." She struggled to not sound breathless, to appear normal.

He'd risen and followed her into the kitchen, closing in on her, reaching—and she reflexively flinched—but he had picked up her plate with the untouched sliver of pie on it, and in a flash, she saw it coming at her face. Quickly turning her head, her hands flying upwards to protect herself, she felt the plate and pie connect with the side of her face. The plate had fallen into her hands, but there would be a bruise on her cheek the next day.

The sudden ringing of the phone in the den saved Martha from further abuse as Ted turned and left, muttering filth. Hearing the door to the small office closing, Martha knew the call would be from a woman. She knew of his affairs and no longer cared. But the call to Shirley would have to be done. She had felt hurt on discovering after marriage how he had really felt about her looks. He had convinced her to change her brown hair to red, and her hazel eyes to brown with colored contacts. He changed her style choice. And he didn't like her family. Contact with friends had gradually melted away. The Christmas card list consisted now of Ted's friends and associates. Her family had become discouraged trying to plan to get together. Invitations she accepted she invariably had to call back and cancel with made-up reasons. Her father had suffered a heart attack and passed away five years earlier. That was the last time she had seen any of her relatives. She begged for a car of her own; an inexpensive used one, but Ted insisted it was an unnecessary expense and that he could take her wherever she needed to go. Only it turned out it was always an inconvenience to him whenever she had somewhere to go, or something to shop for. So, she let her driver's license expire. He had never wanted her to work outside the home, and as months became years, Martha realized she had no skills, no way to sustain herself. And no money. Ted controlled the purse strings and demanded an accounting for every cent she spent. She used the Des Moines bus system for grocery shopping, avoiding frozen produce that melted on the way home; Ted wanted everything fresh anyway.

She was on a bus now, going for the hair appointment Shirley had managed to arrange for her. There had been a time when Ted accompanied her to the beauty shops; watching, restless, foot-tapping until the hairdresser became nervous and eventually dropped her as a client. Eventually he had told her "Take a bus—I'm busy."

Shirley, though, hadn't missed what was going on and was relieved for Martha when she began showing up without the heavy presence of her husband. Gradually, the two women became friends, and under Shirley's warm inclusiveness, Martha began to relax and enjoy her time in the beauty shop. Recently, Shirley had handed Martha a mirror, and tipping Martha's head until she could see the hair roots in a part, the beautician had shown her that the hair was now growing in white.

Tears had stung Martha's eyes. How could this be? She was only thirty-five! The thought that she hadn't even seen her own hair color in over fifteen years was what had brought the tears.

The kind stylist had seen so many women over her years in the business that she had pretty much figured out what Martha's life with Ted must be. Now she cupped her hands on the thin woman's cheeks, avoiding the bruise, and tried to cheer her, saying, "Oh. Marti—you would be beautiful bald! Forget the white!"

The response was unexpected. "No! No—not 'Marti'! He doesn't like Marti. It's Martha!"

"I was right," was all Shirley could think.

As the hair coloring progressed, Shirley had, unnoticed, carefully selected a bottle of matching touchup hair color for her client, and later as the bill was being paid, she had tucked the bottle into a side pocket of Martha's purse and quickly gave her simple instructions on hiding the white line as it grew out. Not for the first time, Shirley took note of the thin wallet with a few small bills, and how Martha always smoothed the receipt and slipped it in behind tens and twenty. Then on the back of a business card Shirley wrote her personal phone number and handed it to Martha. She surprised herself. Never had she done anything like that in all the years she'd had clients. Was she losing her mind? The last thing she wanted or needed was to attract the ire of a man like Ted Sweltzer!!

Outside the salon, Martha paused, looking down at the card for an odd span of time, then slipped it into her slacks pocket, her fingers lingering on the small business card, her thoughts far away.

It would be a while before the next bus made its pickup. Unhurried, Martha walked the few blocks to the bench shielded on three sides in clear plastic for protection from inclement weather for those who relied on the transit system. Several riders already waited by the time she reached the bus stop. She pretended not to notice the two teenagers, obviously a couple from the whispers and laughter. A tired looking woman was seated, so Martha chose to stand as she waited, glancing occasionally at the woman, wondering about her. She wore a work uniform of some sort. Was she a caregiver? Janitorial? She looked dejected, worn. Martha's wandering thoughts served to keep her from dwelling on being back in the "house." She never thought of it in terms of "home."

Scanning the empty seats on the bus, Martha headed towards one that had fewer strangers around her, and gratefully sank onto the seat. She became aware that this bus smelled clean and looked cleaner than some she had been on. Her thoughts inevitably turned back to the house. To the dull, lifeless atmosphere of it—beige-beige-beige. It was like living in a desert. Ted chose the paint. Every wall in every room was beige. As were all the carpets. And not a picture or decoration, aside from lamps, anywhere.

A faint, high-pitched whine broke Martha's concentration.

The sound came again, louder, chilling. It was a sound she'd heard in nightmares too many times. Unable to stop herself, she turned her head towards the sound, and saw the bright, beady eyes of a teacup sized dog peeking out of a young woman's coat pocket. "Look away! Block it out! Don't think about it!" --but all the silent shouts in Martha's head failed. And behind her tightly shut eyes she saw again as clearly as if it were yesterday, the young, stray dog. Light brown, obviously starving, now in her back yard, fearfully begging. It trembled till it shook, its eyes focused on her face as it whined. She'd tried to soothe it in a calming voice, and it had crawled to her, trying to wag the drooping tail, and finally exposing its belly in subservience. She had stroked and petted the pathetic creature until its shaking stopped and it was looking hopefully at her face.

She had gone into the house without thinking ahead. Putting leftover food from the refrigerator into a bowl, she had gone back outside and fed it. Had given it water. It had gratefully licked her hand.

The dog was aware of Ted before Martha was. Sensing something not right, it had pressed its body against her legs, but Ted was fast, and he had the animal by the scruff of its neck before Martha could move or speak. It all happened so fast. Too fast. A few steps and Ted had shoved the shrieking dog into the rain barrel beneath the down spout where rainwater was collected for watering flower beds. Martha had rushed, screaming at Ted, and he had whipped one hand out of the barrel and smashed the back of his fist into her face, lifting her off her feet and hurtling her to the ground.

When she came to, it was to see Ted holding up the drowned dog's limp body. Then he threw it at her. "Now bury it."

She should have left him then. She'd thought about it. Tried to find some way to safely leave. And always she vacillated. Wavered. Gave up. With each surrender, she despised herself more for being so weak, spineless.

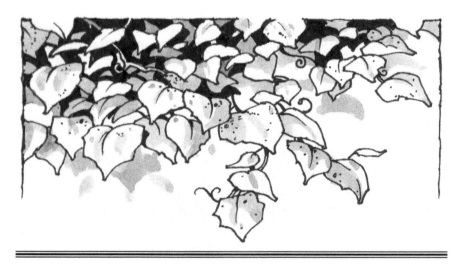

THEODORE WENCEL SWELTZER

Trudging up the sidewalk, Martha could see the white, two-story saltbox style house she called "home" coming into view. She also saw the garage door was up with Ted's new black car parked inside and felt the all-too-familiar sinking in the pit of her stomach.

From the window in the den Ted watched as Martha walked up the drive, noting the hunched shoulders, bowed head, the dragging footsteps, and felt again a niggling uneasiness as he watched. He had always had complete control over her, but something seemed different lately. Ted had the instincts of a hunter who knew his prey, and he didn't like what was puzzling him now. Well, there were ways to deal with it. Right now, other things were on his mind, and he turned his attention to the expensive watch on his wrist. He'd wait an-other five minutes, then call Rachel.

As he heard Martha in the kitchen, he closed the den door knowing she would not disturb him. A fat business envelope lay on his desk where he'd tossed it on coming in. He took a small ring with two keys from an inside pocket of his suit jacket and with one key unlocked the deep bottom drawer on the left side of his desk. Inside was a sizable metal box he opened with the other key, revealing piles of cash grouped in large denominations. He then added the contents of the enve-lope. He owned several rental properties and encouraged cash payments so as to avoid paying taxes. Locking his secret away again, he made his call to Rachel.

He grinned when he thought about her—it had been a hoot seducing the preacher's pretty wife. And not all that difficult. The truth was, she bored him and now had his eyes on a new interest.

Filled with self-satisfaction over his increasing cash boun-ty, as well as his success with attractive women, he reached into the small closet for his golf bag. Ted enjoyed conducting business on the golf course. What he didn't know was Martha knew about his money cache as well as his affairs.

It had been purely accidental discovering Ted was stashing money in the house. She never over-stepped boundaries her husband put in place and she never looked in his desk or into any of his personal belongings.

It had been a warm, sunny day—a good excuse to get out of the house by weeding flower beds. Ted had been in the kitchen as she went out through the garage to weed behind the house. She had seen her husband watching from the window over the sink. Several minutes into the work Martha changed her mind and walked around the garage to the front steps and began trimming back grass along the cement and pulling weeds from around low bushes. On hands and knees, pulling a bag to put clippings and yard waste into, she worked her way along the house foundation to below the window into the den. Taking a breather, she'd sat back on her heels. Then reaching a hand to the low window ledge, began to stand, but was suddenly immobile on finding herself looking directly in at Ted seated at his desk, back to the window.

Time seemed to stand still when she saw him open a large metal box filled with money, to which he was adding more. As she swiftly dropped from sight, she had glimpsed the open bottom left drawer. Within seconds, Martha was again in the backyard, busily weeding the foundation there.

"No wonder it's always cash he hands me for groceries. Never the checkbook. No credit card," was running through her mind.

Memories of Martha's childhood passed through her head as she went about her routines of laundry, cleaning, cooking preparation. Growing up, no one had raised their voices to one another, much less a violent hand. She and her younger sister lived quiet lives in a quiet home where Sunday School and church had been important. Both girls had piano lessons and sang in school chorus. Their father had been a mechanic, a very good one, coming home at night in grease-stained clothes, his hands roughened, and permanently stained in black grease, outlining the fingernails and callouses. He was only fifty-five when he died suddenly. A heart attack. She could still see his stained, workworn hands as he lay in his casket.

She wondered how Ted always knew when she used the phone, and it always provoked him into an argument at the very least, a rage at worst. Martha had quit trying to call her family. Friends no longer called. Nor did her family, and she found it best not to mention them at all. She knew her mother had re-married two years later and had moved to Rochester, MN with her new husband, and Julia. Martha wondered if she would ever meet her stepfather, Harold Bolin. She hadn't bothered letting Ted know these facts. Neither had she told him of the visit from his sisters a little over a year earlier following her mother-in-law's funeral. Peggy and Donna had said their good-byes after the burial and left for their homes. A week later, with Ted at work, the two women had rung Martha's doorbell. "Ted's not here. He'll be home for dinner—why don't you come back then?" She couldn't hide her nervousness over their unexpected presence in Ted's absence. But they'd come determined to see Martha. Alone. The withdrawn, distant sisters-in-law weren't what they had seemed in the ever-present company of their brother. Or father. Hurriedly, now they pleaded with Martha to get help! There were abuse shelters. They talked of what their mother had suffered for so many wasted years. And Ted was just the same as his father. They told her of the neighborhood animals he had abused and killed. They told of his cruelty to themselves he had inflicted. And they talked of their mother's suicide as Martha wept, and pleaded for them to go before Ted came home.

She knew Josey had committed suicide by hanging herself. And that the police had also looked at it as possibly homicide, for a while. Martha hadn't known Josey had hung herself in her husband's closet using one of his neckties.

Ted was in a good mood. His whole day had gone well. Business was good; customers were steady, money was rolling in. And everything was moving in the right direction with his new love interest. And this one had money! Came from money. Nice enough looking, too. "Yes, life is good," Ted thought as he smoothly navigated the evening traffic in his luxury car. He had another envelope of cash for his savings box tonight. The "old man" had no idea Ted had figured out how to enrich himself with no one the wiser. Ted had a collection of mental terms he applied to his father. "Old Man" was the politest.

Martha had heard the car pulling into the drive, and was in the kitchen; makeup in place, long, red hair brushing her shoulders, dressed as though guests were expected. None were. It was what Ted expected to see when he arrived home.

His good mood lasted through the formal dinner, to Martha's relief. Then pouring himself another glass of wine, Ted informed her he had business calls to make, adding he had business meetings scheduled for the weekend and wouldn't be around.

He watched her as he made these pronouncements, trying to read her still face. She seemed different in an unexplainable way. He'd eased up on her food restriction when her boniness drew comments at church, said in jest about him starving her, and he'd been furious about it. Thinking about her was taking the edge off his good mood.

After putting on an apron, Martha fastened the long hair back and removed the irritating brown contacts. Then set about cleaning up after dinner, relieved to know Ted would be occupied for the rest of the evening.

Tired, but too restless to sleep yet, Martha paced the floor of the bedroom, her mind in a turmoil. A warm soak in the tub would have been soothing but being in a tub filled with water was something she never did with Ted in the house. He had nearly drowned her several years earlier when he had come home in a fury when she hadn't answered the phone when he called. She had been outside planting flower beds. Then she had gone for the bath before fixing the evening meal. He had left work and come home early. On finding her in the bathtub, he pushed her head under water and held her there until her lungs burned for air. He would let her up long enough to gasp air, then shoved her under a second time. She believed her life was over and loss of bodily functions had happened which resulted in Ted's releasing her in disgust.

She wished for a book to read, but there were none in the house. If she turned TV on, the sound might irritate him so that was out.

She wondered about church Sunday. If she guessed correctly, Ted wouldn't be around to attend but would no doubt ask Wencel to come by to pick her up. She had never felt comfortable around her father-in-law, and now was less so since Josey's death.

Ted and Wencel had chosen this particular church years ago, with an eye to the one that would be best for business. They had keyed in to where the wealthiest people attended services. Eventually, many of the Sweltzer customers were also acquaintances and golfing friends from that church. Ted had a key to one of the entrances which had seemed strange to Martha since he never volunteered for anything there, nor had he ever been on any board. Recently, she had picked it out of the trash where he'd thrown it.

The affair with the parson's wife was over. For Ted, anyway. He hadn't wasted more than a passing thought on Rachel after he had begun pursuing Audra. For Rachel, the affair would never be over—she was pregnant. Her infatuation with Ted was such she had begun plans to divorce her husband, believing there was a wonderful future waiting for her with Ted. Her reaction on learning of his disinterest in any continuing relationship was, at first, disbelief. Then grief, and torrents of tears, all of which left her formerly attentive lover unmoved. Lastly, rage was all that was left—for all the good that did either. All she could do was try to put her life back together, hoping no one had noticed, or knew, what had been going on behind her husband's back.

But for Ted's new love interest, an attractive little hideaway was quietly rented, and he began wining and dining Audra in earnest.

He had also begun thinking about Martha more lately. Finally, he had learned what was really on her mind. It had been an evening after he'd had a tiring day at work and Martha had irritated the hell out of him for no reason, so he'd slapped her around a little bit. All of a sudden, she'd blurted out they should divorce. Martha wanted to leave, begged to just leave! Who the hell did she think she was! Ted had wrapped an arm across her neck from behind and squeezed till she was passing out. Loosening the pressure, he had whispered into her ear that she'd go when he said so, then slightly increasing the pressure again he had added, "Run if you want! I'll find you and skin you like a rabbit!"

The word "divorce" had been enough to enrage him. The scrawny bitch would never get a penny of his money!

Martha was fully aware of how unimportant she had become to Ted. Her mind felt as though it were filled with skittering mice--her thoughts jumbled together, concentration difficult. Going to the police was out of the question: he had friends in uniform that he made sure she knew about. She still had fears for her family but felt sure he didn't know her mother's new name. At least she believed he didn't know it. And she didn't trust a shelter to be able to protect her.

Pacing didn't solve anything, and she had to put a full spread on the table before it got any later. She tried so hard all the time to not do anything to upset Ted. How tired she was.

Running water at the sink over the vegetables for the salad, she had glanced out the window, scanning the yard. She had been chasing rabbits out of the backyard and into the trees and brush rimming their property. Ted had set a rabbit trap to get rid of them. When she had seen the knife and traces of blood, she knew he had caught one. She began sprinkling pepper on the ground around the trap after that, which had helped. She didn't dare trip the trap for fear of Ted.

More than a week had passed tranquilly with no outbursts from Ted. Most nights he came home late and ignored the food Martha had kept ready and warm for him. She relaxed when he took himself to the den, always closing the door. Occasionally he would catch up on the late news from the area, and Martha breathed a little easier with his attention elsewhere.

But when so many days passed and Ted's behavior remained non-aggressive, Martha began to feel unsettled. Something was going on beneath the surface: a different fear raised its ugly head. He was planning something, and she knew it was nothing good.

The attempted kidnapping occurred mid-morning as Martha pulled the two-wheeled carrier she used to get groceries home. There was no need to hurry, it was a perfect day to enjoy the fresh air and warm sun. She knew the bus schedule and always allowed time for its arrival with no need for rushing about. Traffic was light, rush hour was over, shoppers either still dawdling at home yet, or occupied elsewhere.

An old van passed slowly, only vaguely noted by Martha. Minutes later it had gone by a second time, a little faster, then pulled to the curb not far from in front of her. As she came even with it, the rear passenger door slid open, and too swiftly to process what was happening, a wiry man had sprinted across the grass edge and had pinned Martha's arms to her sides, gripping her from behind and rapidly lifted her off her feet and rushed her towards the open van door. Once again Martha was in an all too familiar struggle to save herself from pain and terror. Only this time it was a stranger's painful grip on her body instead of Ted.

There were a few walkers a little distance from the van, engrossed in their own thoughts until the screams startled, then stopped them in their tracks while they looked about for the source of the screams.

The man gripping Martha was unprepared for such a small woman to fight so fiercely. She had lifted her feet, thrusting them out before her and planted them against the door frame and kicked herself backwards away from the open door of the darkened interior of the van. Her attacker struggled for balance, then freed one hand long enough to land a vicious punch to the side of Martha's head. A passing taxi had stopped in the street and the driver had laid on the horn. One of the walkers, a young man, was on a dead run towards the kidnapper and his victim as Martha heard an angry voice from inside the van yelling, "Get in, get in!" and she felt herself being hurled towards the sidewalk. Then a door slammed, an engine roared and, with tires squealing, the van with Martha's attackers was gone.

The young man who had rushed to help her insisted Martha not move and had knelt beside her asking if she knew the men who had tried to take her. He had awkwardly pulled a wrinkled hanky from a pocket and offered it to her to wipe the tears that streamed down her cheeks, and she used it gratefully. Someone had called the police, and the sirens could be heard coming closer. A few people had gathered, clustered, around her and she heard the shock and outrage in their muffled voices, muttering that "thugs and criminals could walk about and do such horrendous acts—in broad daylight, yet!"

The thought of the police was not comforting to Martha. They were Ted's friends. He would be informed of everything she said! And she could think of no one who would wish her such harm as to kidnap her. Her only enemy was her husband. What had changed, that he could be so different towards her for the past couple of weeks?

She remembered the words, "You'll leave when I say so!"

The police had put her in the patrol car and taken her to the station to get the details and a picture of her swelling cheek bone. She refused to be taken to the hospital. She and the witnesses gave matching descriptions of an old white van with two scruffy men in their mid-to-late twenties. The one who had grabbed Martha wore a brimmed cap pulled low over his forehead, was deeply tanned, and smelled of gasoline. She could not identify him. No one got the license plate number. The police officer who drove her home had seemed a decent sort and appeared genuinely sorry for her ordeal. As he let her out in her driveway, he had encouraged Martha to notify the police if she could recall anything more about the incident. "Anything at all," he had repeated.

His kind sincerity nearly broke her resolve to not tell him her suspicions about her husband. Mumbling a "Thank you," Martha hurried away. And the troubled officer had no doubt in his mind the small, frightened woman had come close to telling him something. He'd thought it odd that she had been adamant that her husband not be called or bothered; that she would let him know the facts that evening. Odd, too, that she seemed to have no one else who could be called.

That night Ted came home from work early—and in a furious mood. The verbal abuse was bad, but at least he had kept his hands off her.

Hardly aware of the food placed in front of him, Ted had eaten rapidly and retreated to his home office, slamming the door behind him.

Sitting motionless at his desk, one hand resting on the phone he thought through what he would be saying to Lonnie and Mort, the two pieces of garbage he'd hired to do a "job" for him. He had hired only one, but the fool had brought in an "assistant" because the bitch never left the house or went where they could grab her unseen. She only went out for groceries at busy times. And Ted had stipulated nothing was to happen at the house or anywhere near the vicinity. Laughing, he had added, "Do whatever you want with her. Just make sure she's never found."

A story would have to be concocted for his police buddies to explain away the failed attempt that had happened. What he came up with sounded plausible as he spoke to himself in low tones. "Martha's the size of a schoolgirl--must have been pedophiles. Probably thought the kid was running errands for her mother and grabbed her on impulse. Doesn't look planned out to me."

That should distract suspicions from himself if the cops started looking further. Only now he would have to wait before he could move ahead with his plans. Martha had become an impediment.

Audra wasn't the type to accept being hidden, meeting in the small apartment. As nice as it was, it would become unacceptable to her before long. And Ted didn't want this fish to get away. He had finished an angry talk with his hirelings, putting everything on hold regarding Martha.

He dialed Audra and his voice changed, becoming low, smooth; and he carried on a lengthy, seductive conversation with the unsuspecting woman who believed she had finally met her "prince."

The feeling of something bad pending lurked in the shadows of Martha's troubled mind. Keeping her in an unsettled state. She had always been good at keeping things together no matter how bad things might get. But now she felt jittery, and afraid of the shadows in her own home, unable to follow-through on anything. She hadn't been able to sleep for several nights, and she was exhausted. Four days had passed since the horrifying abduction attempt had happened to her.

Sitting listlessly at the breakfast table, Martha had watched Ted carrying his briefcase as he left for his work. Wearily her eyes wandered over the kitchen mess, then picking up her plate of untouched eggs and bacon, she dumped it in the trash and put the plate into the sink—with a clatter and left a small stream of hot water running over the stuck food. Toast and coffee were all her stomach could tolerate. Looking around at the disorder, Martha set Ted's breakfast dishes back on the table, leaving the mess, and tiredly made her way back to an unmade bed. She lay down, pulling the blankets around her neck as she turned on her side curling into a ball and closed her eyes. Trying to empty her mind of every thought Martha eventually drifted into welcome rest—free of nightmares.

Waking hours later and realizing the day had slipped away with nothing in order or the evening meal begun, Martha's anxiety returned with a vengeance and she rushed through dressing, putting the bed in order before hurrying to the kitchen where Ted's breakfast dishes still sat with dried on food. Picking up the dishes but distracted by the shadows of the trees outside marking the lateness of the afternoon, her eyes had gone directly to the hated cage--she dropped the plate and cup on the ones in the sink, breaking several pieces, with the small stream of water--now cold, still running over them. She had forgotten to re-apply pepper after the recent rain. "Dear God! Please, no..." was Martha's prayer-like reaction when she saw the rabbit in Ted's trap.

In that moment, something changed for Martha. A line had been crossed. There would be no going back. Silently, but swiftly she exited the kitchen, into the garage where she took a hammer from the hook that kept it on the pegboard. She had to take the time to unlock the door at the back of the garage, but outside she knelt beside the cage, unlocking it and then distanced herself until the terrified animal found its escape and raced into the undergrowth among the trees. And Marti whispered, "Run. Run..."

Bending to pick up the hammer she had dropped by the cage, Marti raised it over her head, and using all the force she had, she brought it down over and over again, smashing the hated cage until it could never be restored. With the hammer, still in her hand, she returned to the garage, to the tool bench looking for something. The something was a large screwdriver.

A decision had been made at long last! Purposefully, and swiftly, Marti passed through the messy kitchen, unmindful of the water still running in the sink. Entering Ted's forbidden office, moving around the desk, she stopped in front of the two drawers on the left. There she knelt and with the hammer and the screwdriver, Marti utterly destroyed the large bottom drawer, then dragged out the metal cash box.

Again, with hammer, screwdriver, and fierce determination the contents of Ted's box were soon in Marti's hands. Thinking fast and clearly now, she placed most of the bills in bundles, keeping out several hundred. The bundles went into plastic sandwich bags she rubber-banded shut.

The feeling of urgency was almost overwhelming. Marti knew every minute counted if she was to escape her cage. No one would be coming to help her. Run! Run! Marti picked up the pace, disrobing in the upstairs bathroom where she taped the plastic bags of cash around her thin body. Forcing herself to be calm, Marti dressed in dark slacks and a loose dark top, then slipped dark socks and good walking shoes onto her feet. Pulling her long hair into a ponytail, she struggled to get it all under a brimmed hat but gave up and found one of Ted's dark caps in his closet which was larger and finally the red hair was out of sight. The hated contacts she flushed down the toilet, her sunglasses she retrieved from her purse and put with her wallet now filled with cash into an old fanny pack found at the back of a closet shelf. Ready to leave, Marti had reached the bedroom door before she remembered there was something else that couldn't be left for Ted to find. Turning back, she raced to her bedside table, opened the drawer and lifted out an old, framed photo of her parents. Beneath was a worn album. This she began flipping through until mid-way she stopped and pushed her fingers behind a larger size photograph to pull out the last letter her mother sent her, telling of her re-marriage to a Harold Bolin. They now lived in Rochester, Minnesota, and included was the new address and phone number. Slipping the letter into a pocket she quickly picked up her parents' picture, removed it from the frame and put it with the letter.

Almost flying down the stairs now, wild to be out of the

backyard where no one could witness her leaving. Marti was reaching to open the kitchen door to the garage when she heard the car turning into the drive. Ted was early!

Spinning around and dashing from the kitchen, and down the hall, she turned at the base of the stairs into the seldom-used living room and frantically unlatched the French doors to the dust-filled, never used screened-in porch taking care to close the French doors behind her. The porch screen door hadn't been opened for such a long time and Marti worked at the lock in mounting desperation. When it finally released and Marti was out of "the cage," running as if the hounds of hell were snapping at her heels. "Run, Marti--run!"

Preoccupied with thoughts of Audra and exploring ways in which he could induce commitment from her, Ted knew he couldn't move too fast, or he'd lose her. Audra was no one's fool. She was not unaware her money had a way of making her extra-attractive to more than just Ted and he liked the future he pictured for himself with her in his mind. He liked the prospects too much to make any stupid moves.

Mentally planning his evening after enjoying the Faroe Islands salmon he'd told Martha to fix, he parked his car and entered the kitchen, looking forward to a pre-dinner glass of his favorite chardonnay as he changed into more casual clothing.

The kitchen door had scarcely closed behind him before Ted was immobilized as he surveyed the messy kitchen with no sign that his dinner was in progress.

"Martha!" came out from his mouth as a roar and, hearing no response, he had rushed furiously through the kitchen shouting. "Where the hell are you?" Fury burned in him, and he was cursing foully, and threatening her if she didn't appear immediately. Very few people knew Ted was exceptionally foulmouthed. He was skilled in hiding behavior that would turn others' approval away from him. He had perfected the art of concealing what would work against him. Now he stood at the foot of the stairs, listening intently for any sound Martha might make. Turning his head from one side to the other, he saw nothing out of place, but then very faintly he caught the sound of water running somewhere--seemed to be the kitchen. Retracing his steps, Ted stopped before the sink, looking down at broken breakfast dishes with a thin stream of water running over them. Stretching out one hand towards the handle marked "hot," he touched the stream of water with the other. Cold. The water had to have been on all day.

Puzzled now, and trying to think what could have happened, he turned the water off and after another look at the broken dishes began slowly walking down the hall. It was too still. "Something's happened to her," he thought. "Could she have fallen? What--? Maybe she's...," his thoughts trailed as he continued his searching.

A careful sweep of his eyes around the living room showed nothing out of place. A glance into the den showed nothing wrong either. The damaged drawer of his desk faced the window. All Ted could see was the polished front side facing the door.

Speaking now in a normal voice, with an ugly hope surfacing in his mind, he took his time climbing the stairs, occasionally calling her name, glancing into the unused bedrooms as he passed. Reaching the bathroom, he saw Martha's work clothes and shoes lying on the floor. Strange. The master bedroom was last, but again, no Martha. And nothing looked different here either, except the door to his closet stood open, and for one moment Ted felt a chill go down his spine as he remembered what his mother had done. Hesitantly, but with a macabre eagerness he turned the light on in his closet and saw—nothing out of the ordinary. Nothing!

Then rage and curses exploded again, and he raced downstairs. Ted, for once, was not in control of the situation. A bad situation. He paced as he gathered his thoughts, sometimes thinking out loud. After the botched kidnapping, the police would be suspicious if he reported the bitch missing now.

Surely Lonnie and Mort hadn't gone ahead on their own and come to Ted's home after being told to get lost until further notice. He had no choice but to call Mort.

This time Ted rounded his centrally placed desk bringing the smashed drawer and empty money box into view, so shocking him that he staggered before he dropped on a knee to reach for the empty box. Picking it up, he looked into it as if to make his missing cash reappear.

And then Ted screamed, hurling the empty box at the wall, smashing a hole through the wall board. With an unsteady hand he rolled his desk chair out and shakily sank into it.

Out loud in an expressionless voice came the words, "I will kill her. I will skin her alive when I catch her if it's the last thing I do." She had the whole day to get a head start on him, or so he believed. He began to construct a plausible story for her disappearance. He could make it look like she had run off with another man. He'd pull it off somehow. First, he needed to find a suitcase. Those were in the basement and he moved quickly, after closing the office door behind him.

He'd found a large suitcase and taking it up to the bedroom opened it on the bed. In Martha's closet, he chose her nicer outfits suitable for the season and heaped them into the suitcase. Shoes followed. Then Ted began gathering Martha's undergarments and sleepwear from her chest of drawers.

Looking around and trying to think what a woman would pack for a trip, he picked up her small jewelry case with her costume jewelry. He knew well there was nothing of value in it and tossed it on top of the pile of clothing.

In the bathroom, looking around, Ted gathered what makeup, lotions, and perfumes Martha most likely used, then added a comb, brush, and toothbrush. Returning to the suitcase he forced everything in and zipped it.

It was heavy and he dragged it down the stairs and out to

the garage where he left it by the car until darkness had fallen.

Late in the night, after making sure no one was loitering about in the neighborhood to wonder what he was up to, he had opened the garage door and then the car trunk lid. Lifting the heavy suitcase into the back wasn't easy.

A short while later he was driving over a bridge on the Des Moines River making sure there were no witnesses. Then returning, he stopped just long enough to force the suitcase over the railing as fast as he could.

It made for a late night for Ted with little sleep and an empty stomach. Morning brought no improvement to his foul mood as he gave up finding anything for his breakfast. He would have to settle for a deli or fast-food place, all of which didn't match up to what he had become accustomed to and believed he was entitled to.

MARTI

What in the world had she been thinking? What had come over her? Marti had run, as long as she could, through brush and trees until her lungs burned and she had no choice but to stop for air and rest. It was too light yet to go out to the streets. Ted could be out, driving around, searching for her. Darkness could hide her. So, she sat on the ground with her back against a tree trunk, waiting for the concealment of the night.

Marti waited, eyes watching for any movement, ears tuned to the sounds of nature mingling with muted car traffic and an occasional horn. Somewhere a dog barked. As she waited, shadows deepened until at last she rose, ready to risk mixing with fellow humans, before it was too dark to find her way out of the wasteland that meandered through the uneven, over-grown terrain behind the quite-nice homes. Similar to the one she had just run from. Carefully picking her way, she hid beneath the overhanging trees at the edge of a yard behind a house with dark windows, alert for any movement—emerged cautiously, silently onto a sidewalk, following it casually to a corner. There, by the help of yellow streetlight, she recognized where she was and breathed a sigh of relief that she had gotten as far as she had from Ted. She knew where she was going, that a bus would be needed to get her there.

Streetlights and car headlights shone outside the bus windows as Marti made herself as small and unnoticed as possible, her right hand in the jacket pocket, fingers wrapped around a sharp-edged palm-sized rock for self-defense which she found on her way through the brush and ravines. Her eyes, shadowed beneath the hat brim, noted the passing street signs and she chose an un-peopled corner to disembark. Moving purposefully down a tree-lined street, she made several changes in direction until the familiar shape of the large stone-sided church she had attended so many years came into view. No one was about as she slipped behind the great hedge growing along the sidewalk.

The streetlight didn't reach into the recessed side door leading to the office area. From the pocket holding her parents' photo, Marti withdrew the key Ted had thrown away, and holding her breath, fumbled the key into the lock. At the sound of the click she exhaled and carefully turned the knob, then slipped into the dark interior locking the door behind herself. Not moving but listening intently with the rock again tight in her fist, she waited, willing her eyes to adjust to the darkness. She knew her way about the elegant old church but wished she had something to light her way. Impossible to turn any light on—someone would see and report it. And the police were not her friends, they were Ted's.

Slowly feeling her way to the custodian's small room, she hoped to find a flashlight, or even a candle and matches. The secretary's office would be locked, but surely not the custodian's room. Luckily, it was not.

Faint light from two high windows directed streetlight into the small room bringing some relief from the darkness. The search took time, but what else did she have to make demands on her now anyway? No meals or dirty dishes. No laundry to tend to. Nothing.

She was identifying things by feel and recognized the shape of a box of wooden matches. Carefully striking a match and keeping more ready, she searched faster and found the stub of a candle in a drawer. Better! Easier to look around now.

Inside a metal cabinet Marti found the sought-after flashlight, and then extinguished the candle putting it and the matches back in their places. She was careful not to bring attention to anything out of place that would be noticed should anyone come in when the day came. Police were something she did not want to attract. It was the weekend. No one should be coming into the church unless it would be the custodian completing some undone job before Sunday. Aiming the light to the floor as much as possible, Marti made her way downstairs to a kitchen area and began a search of the refrigerator for anything that would stave off the hunger pangs she felt. Empty—except for a large bottle of unopened orange juice, surrounded by bottles and jars of pickles, ketchup, mustard, relishes, and jams. Carrying the juice to the counter, a search began for paper cups, which was helpful in finding crackers, as well. Not what she had hoped for but certainly better than nothing. Returning to the refrigerator, Marti opened the freezer section and found frozen cupcakes and cookies, from which she helped herself quite generously.

Grateful, as well as feeling better, Marti began making her way to where the women usually held their meetings, and there she collected two throw pillows from the sofa, then continued towards the front of the church--adding to her collection a coat left hanging in the lost and found. It should not be missed if anyone did come in.

The belfry had a velvet rope across the stairway with a "Do Not Enter" sign hanging on it. The bell had been disengaged due to deterioration. Restoration was being discussed.

Marti made her way up the winding staircase to a second level landing hoping with all her heart the custodian would have no reason to come up there and find her. It was not going to be an easy night's rest on the hard wood floor, but there was no other way at least not for this night. If Ted had reported her missing, the police would be checking motels, hotels, and bus stations—nowhere felt safe to her. If she could stay here until sometime late Saturday, it would give her time to figure out how to get out of the city unseen. Or unrecognized.

Right now she felt so tired. Maybe sleep would come despite the uncomfortable accommodations. Then settling in the best she could, Marti closed her eyes and gave a sigh. She ached with tiredness and, longing for sleep, emptied her mind of all disturbing thoughts, determined to find rest. It appeared to work for a while before the thought drifted in of the last time she had been to church. Was that last Sunday? Her thoughts seemed so jumbled since the horrible episode on her way home from the grocery store. And with that memory, sleep fled. She moved restlessly, forcing herself to fix her mind on simpler details, calling up things she had memorized at one time or another. As a child she'd had a Sunday School teacher who had the children memorize Bible verses. Now she began searching her memory, slowly bringing up one verse, then another. She had been required to know a hundred verses by the time of her confirmation. How could she have forgotten so many—or could they still be locked away somewhere in her head? When the words "The Lord is my rock, my fortress, and my deliverer," flowed through her mind, Marti sat up, her back against the wall—she knew those verses from the last time she had attended church. They were in Psalm 18—and she had nearly wept as the minister read the scripture about the "cords of death entangling," of God "hearing the cries"; and "rescue from powerful enemies." Of being brought out into "a spacious place."

"Oh! That He would free her from her cage of Ted's control," had filled her mind that morning with such a depth of longing.

She slept fitfully, to no surprise but was fully awake as soon as the darkness began to lessen. She felt stiffness and sore muscles almost everywhere. No need for the flashlight now but felt a sense of urgency to hurry with washing up in the ladies' room. Her hair was a mess which she could only finger comb, then pull back into a ponytail, and jam the cap back on. She made a return visit to the kitchen for a breakfast of crackers and orange juice. This time she took the bottle of juice that was left and the entire container of cupcakes and cookies with her as she left the kitchen. It was going to be a long day. Making a split-second decision as she passed the women's meeting room, she made a fast stop, and carried away a book to help pass her time of waiting in the belfry for evening to come again. No one had come into the church all day, but she still hadn't been able to concentrate on the book long enough to follow it and had finally given up. On a careful and fast trip for water, and to the bathroom, Marti returned the book, and scurried like a hunted animal back up the restricted stairs. She hoped Ted assumed she was miles away by now.

She knew what she had to do, and by eight p.m. began to hide all traces of her presence, returning the now wrinkled coat, and tossing cake wrappers, paper cups and juice bottle into the kitchen waste bin.

As she passed the free-will offering box in the Narthex beside small devotionals, Marti stopped and removed her engagement and wedding rings. The diamond would need to be pawned, the gold wedding band she dropped in the free-will offering box with the thought: "I'm free! And it's my will!"

Then by the light of the flashlight she was again in the custodian's small office to use the phone there. Seating herself at the small desk, with trembling fingers she dialed a number she had memorized. It rang several times and Marti's heart sank. On the fourth ring, a familiar voice answered, and in a whisper, Marti said, "Hello, Shirley?"

There was a quick intake of breath on the other end of the line, then, "Who is this?"

Making the whisper louder, she had answered, "This is Marti. Will you help me, Shirley? Right away? I'm hiding. I have to get away from Ted—he's dangerous, Shirley. I need help."

Her friend's answer was clear. "Yes, what is it you want me to do?"

Marti's response was "I need help to get out of Des Moines. Can you help me with that?"

Shirley had been brave enough to answer with, "Yes. Tell me what to do."

It was almost nine p.m. when Shirley drove slowly into the church parking lot near the side door and Marti darted from the shadows to the passenger door almost before the car had reached a full stop. Then the car was again in motion, but to any observer, should there have been one, there was no appearance of anyone being in a hurry.

Marti was desperate that Shirley know everything; to know helping her could put Shirley in trouble or, worse yet, danger from Ted. In the privacy of the car on the Hebner's driveway, Marti's story was poured out for the first time, in a flood of tears--not knowing how this woman would receive or react to all she was hearing. The two women discussed an abuse shelter which Marti rejected knowing that would be the first place a search by Ted, or the police, would be made. To get as far from the city as fast as possible was all Marti wanted. She asked Shirley to buy her whatever she needed to travel, and then to get her to a bus station located somewhere outside Des Moines. Marti held nothing back, telling her helper of the money while the tears still fell. Tissues were pressed into her hands, and a promise was made by Shirley that all the things divulged by Marti would be kept a secret, no matter what.

With the basics of a plan to help Marti, the women went into the Hebner home where Marti was introduced to the kind Ben Hebner, Shirley's husband, a gentle giant of a man who would prove to be as good a secret-keeper as his tenderheart-ed wife.

Food was offered to Marti, and gratefully consumed. A nightgown and robe of Shirley's enveloped Marti, following a warm and welcome shower. Ben's booming laugh erupted at sight of her, and his comment that she looked like a child play-ing in grown-up clothing made everyone laugh. That night Marti slept like a baby in the Hebner's spare bedroom.

Around the Sunday morning breakfast table, the talk turned to changing Marti's look, and Ben had excused him-self, taking the Sunday paper and disappearing in the direc-tion of the living room.

"I wondered what was happening to you after that article in the newspaper, Marti." It was said hesitantly by Shirley, unsure of the response this subject might bring. I tried twice to call, but no one picked up the phone." Changing the topic, Shirley the beautician took over as she ran her fingers through the long red hair and asked Marti if she wanted to go natural or some other color? Long, short, or somewhere in between. Whatever was needed, Shirley would be making a shopping run as soon as a list was compiled.

The day had begun dark and dreary which turned into wind and rain with little let up until towards evening.

Shirley had returned from the shopping soaking wet despite using an umbrella. The wind had sent the rain pelting her skirt and legs and turning the umbrella wrong side out. But she had come back with a triumphant smile, two pairs of dark slacks and tops, a nice concealing jacket—dark, and pajamas. All of which fit Marti, plus a brimmed hat that looked nice with everything. Ted's money had been put to good use.

The ever-thoughtful Shirley had apparently considered everything as she spread out the collection of comb, brush, mirror, toothbrush and small-sized toothpaste, shampoo, and soap. Even the carryall was light weight and could be pulled on two wheels—Shirley had thought of everything.

"Natural," had been Marti's choice for her hair, eliminating the need for frequent hair appointments. And the hairstyle was to be very short. Never again would her hair be long or colored.

The haircut was easy. Stripping the color was harder as well as messy, especially out of the convenience of the beauty shop setting. But at last, the chemicals and color had been rinsed down the kitchen sink and Marti stood holding a mirror looking at her own face as though she looked at a stranger, which oddly wasn't far from what she felt. Huge hazel eyes stared out of a thin pixyish face framed in completely white hair. The short cut had brought out soft waves.

The following day the decision had been made for Shirley to go to the beauty shop as usual. The less she knew of where Marti got on a bus the better. Ben had done the work of getting bus schedules from several nearby towns. And Ben would be the one to drop Marti off without knowing where she was heading. Newton bus depot was her choice of departure.

The evening had been especially subdued, and Marti gave the Hebners her mother's phone number asking Shirley to tell her mother only what was necessary, and to explain to her for the safety of them all there could be no contact, but that when possible she would get a message to her mother. She sent her love to them through Shirley, and then reminded the Hebners to keep their identity from her mother.

She had cried saying goodbye to Shirley the next morning, who hugged her and made her promise to keep in touch. Then she was in Ben's truck and headed for Newton, where Marti received a bear hug from the big man, and a gruff, "You stay in touch now, hear?" Then he was gone and the aloneness that swept over her seemed almost more than she could bear. Pulling the small suitcase and wearing the fanny pack around her waist where the sacks were again taped, Marti began again the "fading-into-the-woodwork" persona. The new cap hid most of the white hair, sunglasses hid her eyes.

Ticket in hand, Marti boarded the bus searching for the seat with fewest people nearby.

The back of the bus appeared least crowded, but surprisingly there were quite a few travelers. Most of those already seated paid little attention to those making their way down the aisle, signaling their wish to not be bothered. One or two raised their eyes briefly in curiosity as Marti passed.

She found an empty row near the back and stowed her wheeled carryall in the overhead space before dropping herself into the first seat, hoping the second seat would go unnoticed. Marti didn't like small talk. Over the years she had grown accustomed to silence. Now she made herself as invisible as possible.

The sound of tires humming on pavement had become almost hypnotic as the time and miles passed. A few low voices droned sporadically among strangers confined to a small space, politely trying to pass the dragging time until they reached their various destinations.

Marti was unaware of the watchful eyes taking in the small form whose face stayed averted, the head tilted slightly down. Eyes hidden behind the dark glasses and hat brim, sitting so still, as if waiting.

Inside Marti's head emotions were rampant: fear of what was behind her, fear of all that was before her, fear of the unknown. Fear of being alone. Or not being alone. Where would she be by nightfall? And what about work? She needed to work. But at what? Shifting to straighten out her legs, and back, she placed a hand on the vacant seat at her side and felt something under her fingers. Turning to look, she saw it was only a small booklet with a pretty pastoral scene on its cover. She picked it up, taking in the green meadow beside a silvery stream, a mountain in the background. It was titled, "The Upper Room." Familiar. She had seen that title before. Where?

Randomly opening the booklet her eyes fell on the topmost line, "I will not forget you." –Isaiah 4:14. And unexpectedly she felt warm tears trickle down her cheeks. Raising first one arm, then the other, Marti used her jacket sleeves to dry her face, and read the five words again. Turning the page, it was Isaiah—again—30:15, "In quietness and trust is your strength." Marti slipped the booklet into a pocket as her jumbled thoughts quieted, and as the miles slipped past, Marti felt hope, strong and clear, for the first time in so many years, and thought, "I'm going to be all right."

Across the aisle from Marti, observant eyes watched, and the old woman smiled to herself.

TATE OSBORN

Officer Osbourn sat at his desk staring down at papers covering the attempted kidnapping from almost two weeks earlier. Nothing had come to light on the case. Odd, too, that the victim's husband hadn't shown much interest in pursuing answers to the "who" and "why" of it. The man had come to the station when asked but had no idea why the incident had happened other than the "perps" could have been pedophiles. His wife could pass for a schoolgirl. She was small, and with the long red hair must have caught their attention. Other than that, he had no idea who would want to harm her.

Leaving the interview, Osbourn had observed the husband of Martha Sweltzer talking with, and glad-handing two of his officers. Osbourn had an uneasy feeling of something just "off" about it all. Or could it be he just didn't like the man. The fear in the victim's eyes stayed with the officer. He felt instinctively the woman wanted to tell him something at the time he'd dropped her back at her home. He decided to check up on her before his shift ended. Maybe she'd recalled something more by now.

As planned, Officer Osbourne had pulled his police cruiser up to the curb in front of the neat, white, two-story classic house and took his time getting out of the vehicle, all the while watching the windows from behind his dark glasses. No movement anywhere was noted as he moved casually up the driveway to the walk leading to the front door. The garage door was closed. He pushed the button by the door and heard chiming somewhere within the house. He waited a few seconds and pushed the button again, getting the same results. Moving off the front stoop his glance took in the first window to his right and casually he moved towards it, then bending at the waist and cupping hands around his eyes, he stared into what appeared to be a small office of some sort.

About to move on around the house to have a look at the backyard he noticed the darkened area on the wall near the door. Odd. Looked out of place. Not a picture. Or mirror. A moment later he knew it was a hole in the wall. A closer look into the room and Osbourn saw the missing drawer from the bottom left side of the desk, and he knew something had happened in this room that needed an explanation.

Walking more quickly he crossed the drive and rounded the garage till he arrived to where he could have a good look at the back yard, edged by trees, thickets, and brush. Except for a smashed cage of some sort, nothing looked out of place. And still no movement at any window. Osbourn knew Martha Sweltzer didn't drive and didn't work outside her home. Where was the woman?

Approaching the steps leading up to a screened in porch, he paused, thoughtfully studying the overgrown brush growing right up to the porch, obviously never used. The wood of the steps near the ground appeared to be deteriorating. Carefully Officer Osbourne examined the overgrown bushes crowding the steps and found two small branches snapped and hanging wilted. Stepping cautiously and using his handkerchief he tested the doorknob and found it unlocked. Within seconds he was inside a dusty unused porch with dirt covered table and chairs. Studying the floor, he saw evidence of footprints leading out of the house. None leading in. Avoiding stepping in the small prints, the officer, again using his hanky, pressed down the handle of the French door where footprints had apparently paused. To close the door he wondered. The French door was also unlocked.

He needed to be talking with some of the neighbors. It would be interesting to hear neighbors' opinions about the couple occupying this house.

By the time Osbourn was back on the drive, a curious neighbor woman had appeared on her drive only a few feet away watching him.

Officer Tate Osbourn was a perceptive man, and it was rare for him not to win over reluctant witnesses. Greeting the older woman pleasantly, he introduced himself, approaching her in a relaxed manner.

When he asked how she was doing, the answer came fast. "I'm doing fine. And it's about time someone came to see how that poor woman's doing!"

The hair literally rose on Osbourn's neck. "Uh, yes. No one's answering the door. Have you seen her leave, ma'am?"

"I haven't seen her in days. Or heard her either." There was an almost angry tone to the woman's voice when she spoke.

"When did you last speak with her, then?" This question seemed to offend her as she snapped back with, "I didn't say that! She never socialized with anyone. But we heard her screams, begging him to stop!"

When asked if she had ever reported what sounded like

assault and abuse, her answer was, "My husband said not to get involved. That Ted Sweltzer is a real mean man. Besides, others heard it, too."

Thanking the neighbor and taking her name, the officer sat in his cruiser giving details and information to headquarters. A woman, victim of a recent kidnap attempt, now appeared to be missing.

Osbourn pulled up phone numbers for Sweltzer's business and called Ted, precipitating an angry exchange. Ted saw no reason why the police should be snooping around his home embarrassing him in front of his neighbors. When asked where his wife was Sweltzer spat out, "The bitch has a boyfriend. She's somewhere with him and I couldn't care less. We were divorcing anyway."

Ted was furious to have police going through his home, checking up on him and demanding explanations, but he wasn't given a choice since he couldn't produce Martha as proof that all was well. It hadn't helped when the matter of his mother's death was mentioned.

On learning of the unlocked doors in the living room and porch Ted realized Martha must have still been there when he drove in. The need for revenge he felt was owed him against her was poison throughout his entire being.

Officer Osbourn hadn't forgotten the glad-handing scene between Ted and two of his own officers.

With search warrant in-hand, Osbourn brought a female police officer with him who could look at the missing woman's home through the eyes of a woman. Together they examined Martha's home and belongings, putting together a fairly accurate picture of her and her life with Ted as possible.

The results were disappointing. Ted stuck to the boyfriend story, but when it came to the smashed desk, he admitted he kept cash handy there (though he lied about the amount), and his fury lent credence that Martha—and the boyfriend? —had left with the money. A boyfriend would have been necessary to haul out the large suitcase that Ted claimed was missing, along with Martha's clothing.

When it came to the unlocked doors and Martha's footprints in the dirt, Ted lost his temper again shouting, "Why not? She lived here!"

There was more negative fallout to come for Ted, further fueling Ted's need for revenge. His new "love," Audra, dumped him so fast after all the negative news press, it was impossible to defend himself to her or to give his own spin on everything to bring her around to his side. He was not used to losing. Marti would be punished for stealing his money, but also for being the catalyst that robbed him of his cushy future with Audra. But Ted now added Audra to his list of those needing punishment. And he knew where to find Audra.

Ted lost not only the secret stash of money, followed by the exit of Audra because of Martha, but when she left, she took with her all that Ted had taken for granted. Expected, really. He had lost his personal slave. When he got up in the morning, he had no clean clothes to put on, he had to go out to find his breakfast, lunch, and dinner. And he hated wading through his own disorder and dirt. He felt as if everything was collapsing around him.

He sold his big house and moved into the former hideaway he'd shared with Audra. And began planning how to find the one person he blamed for his wrecked life. Martha.

GIL AND THORA IVERSON

A neon light outside of Marti's motel window flickered throughout the first night in her new location. Decorah. Not as far as she wanted to be, but in her heart, she knew she needed to be close enough to what family she had. Just not so close as to put Ted's attention on them.

The room cost more than she wanted to pay, but it had been the one closest to the bus depot, so she had walked the short distance and paid its price. When the feelings of panic threatened, Marti thought about the booklet she'd found on the bus; she mentally repeated the words of comfort that were written in it, and calmness would return.

Sleepless in the flickering light of the room, Marti planned her cover story knowing one would be necessary. As much as she didn't want one, it would have to hold together; simple and believable. She decided to use her maiden name, glad her mother had remarried, keeping her safer from Ted. She would say she was separated from her husband, "Frank" and that they lost everything due to his gambling. That they had moved around a lot, and St. Louis had been the last place, when she had left him. Over and over, she rehearsed her story until it came out smoothly with no hitches.

Towards morning, sleep had come, and Marti slept later than she planned. Breakfast would be skipped. She had to be out of the motel before checkout time or pay for another night. She had handwashed the clothes worn the previous day and put them on hangers to dry in the bathroom the night before. Now dried, she packed them into the carryall, then putting on the remaining set of clothing, covering her hair with the hat, her eyes with dark glasses, Marti checked out at eleven a.m. and began the walk to downtown Decorah looking for a café for lunch. The more expensive looking eating places she passed by and settled on a small café where she chose the privacy of a booth near the back where she could face the door.

A newspaper had been left beside a finished meal, and Marti picked it up as she passed. A waitress had been quick to take her order for a cup of soup and a half-sandwich. While she waited, she had opened the paper, folding it to the want ads, and began the search for any job that she might be able to do. Nothing. She checked the "For Rent" ads and looked for rooms to rent. Again nothing. Her order arrived, and the soup was exceptionally good, as was the sandwich. Marti's eyes raised uneasily each time someone came into the café, jingling a bell over the top of the door. Business seemed brisk, drawn by good food, apparently.

As she paid her bill, Marti asked the girl at the cash register if she knew of any rooms to rent and received a discouraging, "No—can't think of any."

About to make her way out, a cork board with notes

thumbtacked to it caught her eye and she began quickly scanning each note. "Ford truck for sale." "Free puppies." "Work wanted." And so it went. Another nothing. Turning to leave she heard a customer who overheard her exchange at the cash register say, "You might try the Gilbert Iversons. Their apartment has been empty for some time. They're in the phonebook. Never hurts to ask." And she gave a charming laugh as she added, "Good luck. Tell them Pam sent you."

Watching the pleasant woman walking away, Marti judged from her attire she could probably be someone's secretary.

It was a bit of a walk for Marti, but the area looked respectable, with surrounding quiet neighborhoods, tree-lined streets; and the Iverson's small white house was well-kept on a large tree-shaded yard with what had once been a small horse barn situated towards the back and to the left. A neat, old-fashioned sign dangled on metal rings from an iron bar over the door and swung gently with every breath of the wind. "Chris's Wood Craft" in black lettering on a white background.

Trying to keep her hopes in check, Marti knocked at the front porch door, and waited. Hesitating a moment more, she knocked again, louder. Enough so that it hurt her knuckles, but at least it caused sounds from within that came closer until the door creaked open. Through the screen Marti saw a short, round older woman. Even her face was round, with eyes abnormally magnified by thick lensed glasses. Her gray hair was tightly permed, and neat. Behind her a man appeared, almost as short as the woman, and equally round with suspenders stretched over a generous stomach, his bright eyes fastened on Marti. And not a hair on his head. They looked Marti over, curiosity written on their faces as they observed the carryall at her side. They seemed a pleasant pair. Marti introduced herself and gave as simple an explanation possible of how and why she had appeared on their doorstep. Saying to them that Pam had sent her had the magical effect of causing two faces to light up simultaneously and two happy voices began talking over each other, telling her that Pam was their granddaughter. The couple interrupted each other, and even finished each other's sentences. Marti felt an urge to laugh.

Then with regret on both their faces Marti heard them say they hadn't decided what to do about the apartment; that having a stranger about might not be such a good idea for them at their ages. Their eyes lingered on what they could see of Marti's face, and they noted the droop that came to the stranger's shoulders. Quietly Marti thanked the couple, gripped the handle of the carryall, and turned to leave. It would have to be the motel again that night.

"Hold on a minute, Miss. Let's talk about this." The elderly man had called out to Marti, stopping her in her tracks. The man seemed to have surprised his wife, but she appeared happy about it.

"Come in, come in," she chirped. And the roly-poly couple led Marti through to a charming kitchen filled with the aroma of fresh baked apple pie, and she felt an instant mouth-watering response.

Marti spent a second night at the over-priced motel while Thora and Gilbert cleaned out Henry's former quarters. The apartment had been the loft in the barn, which Gilbert and his bachelor brother, Henry had finished into a small living area with an entrance at the back of the barn. A railed deck spanned the entire back where Henry liked to sit in the evenings. Inside was a kitchenette/sitting room, and in the bedroom a bathroom with a shower and closet which completed the happy arrangement between the two brothers with opposite personalities. Gilbert took advantage of the opportunity to make further use of the barn and installed a door into the lower portion beneath the deck. His retirement from his career of teaching high school music had been approaching, and thoughts of a woodworking hobby had appealed to him. Over time, he and Henry had turned the barn into a workshop with a small office area at the back with a bathroom installed below the one in the loft. All a nice plan except for the fact that Gilbert didn't really have all that much aptitude for, or dedication to, woodworking.

But the apartment was the perfect solution for Henry. As much as Thora cared for her good-natured brother-in-law, she drew the line on letting him live with Gilbert and her. Henry was a slob. A tobacco chewing, beer-drinking, snore-like-a-buzz-saw congenial bachelor. With a bad "ticker." He had died sitting in his rocking chair, enjoying the evening out on the deck several months before Marti showed up.

Thora had assumed correctly that Marti would need sheets, towels and dishes, so had generously washed up everything and left all the essentials for the new tenant to use.

Marti had been forced to use money from the hidden sacks around her middle to pay the first two months' rent, hoping to soon find work to cover her living expenses, and leave the rest of the funds untouched for an emergency.

She was not only deeply grateful for her delightful landlords, but the motel would have greatly exceeded what her rent was.

Henry had a telephone installed in the apartment and Marti had decided to have it hooked up in her name to make job hunting easier. She'd found a money belt at a garage sale on one of her walks to Main Street and now had Ted's money conveniently in that.

Each day that passed found her more settled into a comfortable routine. Marti was making a new life for herself, but still fell asleep each night with the jagged rock beneath her pillow. Fear kept her alert, and prepared, but Isaiah 30:15 kept her calm.

With the help of garage sales and the Methodist clothes closet, Marti's wardrobe would be adequate.

She posted notes offering housekeeping services in many of the business establishments that looked promising, with her phone number. This appeared to be a common practice for the locals.

After several weeks of no response, her phone finally rang, and to Marti's relief she had a small, two-hours-a-week light housework job. It was a foot in the door, at least. An older man had called when his wife had come home from the hospital following a stroke. He had asked to meet with her first, and Marti realized she would need to have a better way to get to different addresses around the city than to walk.

A bike would be the best, though not a perfect solution. Gilbert suggested she go to a bicycle shop that refurbished trade-ins for a good second-hand bike.

Trusting the clerk's judgment, Marti made her choice, and for a small amount more had saddle baskets added behind the seat. She also purchased a padlock and bike chain before riding off for a test run. She hadn't been on a bike in years.

The darkness of the night slowly faded as dawn made its silent entrance in the loft. Marti had been awake for a while watching her furniture slowly materialize, and overhead the barn beams began forming broad dark lines across the A-shaped ceiling. Today would be the day she met with Nels and Emma Rasmusson. Shirley had written a "good character" recommendation letter for Marti the day she left the Hebners, using the beauty shop address and phone number, with the hours she could be reached. Ben thought it best not to have their phone number and home address available if Ted got his hands on them.

The appointment was in the afternoon—two o'clock. How pleasant not having to rush around. Marti's life now had a different pace, a different feel to it. A good feeling. She padded soundlessly to a window, taking in the sun coming through the fall-colored trees. What beautiful color. The bedroom window slid open easily and a fresh, crisp breeze came through the un-curtained window. Henry hadn't bothered with curtains, and

Marti liked it that way—she felt freer with nothing hindering the view of the outdoors.

In a warm sweater and carrying a cup of fresh, hot coffee she walked out on the deck to sink into the weathered outdoor rocker where Henry had enjoyed nature in his own way. Marti loved the freshness of the early morning with the sound of mourning doves close, but unseen. It was a velvet sound.

Her coffee was cooling so she rose to go inside for a refill. Her garage sale coffee pot brewed good coffee after she had cleaned out the stem to the grounds basket.

With fresh cup in hand, she picked up a small booklet with the other and returned to the deck, seating herself at the top step, setting her cup at her side as she opened the current "Daily Bread." It had been at the church clothes closet when she spotted it at the church entrance beside a basket marked, "Free Will Donation" and she had placed a dollar in it.

Minutes had slipped by un-noticed as she sat on the step, her warm cup between her hands. A car door slammed somewhere near making her jump, and she spilled some of the coffee on her knees. It was time to go in anyway and rising she was gone by the time Chris Losinski rounded the corner of the barn and unlocked his office door below where Marti had been sitting.

NELS AND EMMA RASMUSSON

Gilbert had become acquainted with Chris, an ex-GI, new in town, about the time he realized woodworking was not one of his talents. Chris had joined the Presbyterian Church Gilbert and Thora attended, and eventually Chris's efforts to start his own carpentry shop reached Gilbert's ears, and as they say—the rest was history. Chris had become not only the renter of Gil's barn shop, but he and the Rasmusson's had formed a close friendship. The older couple had come to rely on the younger renter, and Chris had become addicted to Thora's cooking and baking. It had turned into a mutually good arrangement for them.

Chris loved his work. The feel and smell of wood was balm to him; and his business was good. Not booming, but good.

He was content. He had an artist's eye for design, turning out keepsake pieces of furniture and his quality work spread by word of mouth. He never tired of being in the workshop among his tools and furniture-in-progress. His mind was active even as he worked his magic with the wood.

In this moment, his mind was on Henry. He missed the guy. "That was one noisy man upstairs," he thought, remembering the heavy footsteps, whistling, always dropping things and banging around. Not a sound from the new resident—almost like nobody there. Seems the Iversons took a liking to her though. He'd had a couple glimpses of her. Small, boyish, couldn't see her face. Thora said something about a failed marriage. So, what's new? He knew all about what that was like.

Overhead, Marti heard the Iversons downstairs renter at work in his shop. The sounds of saw, sander and drill didn't bother her, but hammering did. Not that she would ever complain. Her life now was the best it had been in so many years.

It was time to go to a pawn broker with her diamond. There was still an amazing amount of money left but how long would it last if she needed to keep on the move every couple of years? The diamond would tide her over till more work could be found.

She showered, then dressed in her usual boyish clothes, added the hat and glasses, and was down the steps, taking her bike from under the shelter of the overhead deck, and hurried off hoping for good luck with the ring at the pawn shop.

Worrying solves nothing. A waste of time and energy. Marti was mentally talking herself into putting the approaching interview with the Rasmussons into proper perspective. They needed to know something of who she was before letting her into their home. This couldn't be easy for them either, but she did so dread putting out her made-up background story.

It was lying to people, no matter how necessary on her part, she reminded herself.

The bicycle proved itself a boon in getting her to wherever she needed or wanted to be. Right now, the weather was mild, and it was pleasant being out. A rain slicker was in one of the saddle bags, ready for a rainy day.

Marti wheeled the bike up the narrow walk to the charming entrance of a stucco home. The recessed front door was painted a Nordic blue and flanked on each side by a narrow, high-backed bench for one; both covered in "Rosemalingen" on blue that matched the door. A curtain had moved at a front window as she had approached, and the door opened as she came up the curved steps where Nels Rasmusson invited Marti in.

Soft-spoken, a kindly man, he had a facial tic that became more noticeable when he was stressed. Now he was stressed not only by the helplessness of his wife, but because it was on his shoulders to determine if this stranger in his living room would be someone to trust and rely on. Emma had always been the outgoing, talkative one who dealt easily with things.

Nels moved nervously where he sat on a chair near Emma in a wheelchair. He glanced frequently at his silent wife as he pushed his glasses up on his nose with one finger, something he unconsciously did at regular intervals. He read Shirley's letter of recommendation aloud to Emma.

Marti had removed the dark glasses as she came in and was unaware of how much her eyes revealed her feelings. Nels questioned Marti, where she was from, and how she happened to come to Decorah. Being a perceptive man, Nels recognized the empathy in the gentle eyes of his guest; and, he thought, a sadness. As the interview ended Nels asked his wife if she would be comfortable having Marti coming in once a week to do light housework.

With effort, Emma managed to get a simple "yes" out. A tour of the home followed with Nels stating that the floors, dusting, and cleaning up the kitchen and bathroom were what they needed help with. After showing Marti where cleaning supplies and sweeper were, the two of them chose Friday mornings at nine a.m. for Marti to arrive which was when Nels would leave to do the grocery shopping and any needed errands. That way Emma wouldn't be alone.

Marti had noted other "rosemal" artwork arranged attractively around the home and commented on how beautiful it was. Nels had paused, and after several seconds, in a sad voice said, "Emma painted all of them." As he escorted her out the door, Marti had turned to look at one of the benches again, and Nels' soft voice came, "Yes, those, too."

Her ride back to her "retreat" –which is how she thought of her new residence—was slow as she mulled over the time spent with those two fine people. "How sad," she thought. "Such talent in that woman's hands and it was her dominant hand she lost use of."

Back in her own kitchen, Marti made up a record-keeper in a tablet for the names, addresses, phone numbers, schedules, and the likes and preferences of her first (and hopefully future) clients.

ROXANNE TRUMAN

What posted notes in public places had failed to do in attracting clients, word-of-mouth made up for. The visiting nurse for Emma had observed the raised spirits of Nels and Emma, as well as a spic-and-span orderly home. Word of the much-liked housekeeper for the Rasmussons spread. Before a month had passed, Marti had two more houses to clean. And as with everything in life, one takes the good with the bad.

The happy, fun-loving Sena Dahl was good. Roxann Truman, not so much. Marti had surmised correctly before her interview with Roxann had even occurred, working for the woman would never be pleasant, but until she had built her clientele to the point she could afford to drop her, she would have to bite her tongue and just do as she was told.

Curtis Truman was a lawyer. He and Roxann had met in college and married when she became pregnant. Just into their forties, with their only child, a son, away in college, they lived in the nicest section of town in a large two-story brick home. And Marti knew what to expect having been instructed to come around to the back door for the interview.

Roxann had shown Marti into the kitchen, and with a red-tipped long fingernail pointed to a chair; and Marti took a closer look at the woman who was examining her. The ultra-blue eyes had to be contacts, and she recognized the bleached blond hair, coiffed and lacquered in place. The clothing was expensive and stylish; and the large diamond on her ring finger matched the diamonds on the ear lobes. And she studied Marti with suspicious, distrustful eyes, more interested in her looks than anything she had to say.

In giving her a tour of the house Mrs. Truman stated exactly what she expected, and how everything was to be done, as well as how often Marti was to show up for work and when.

On hearing Friday mornings were filled, Mrs. Truman froze. Then, turning to Marti, coldly stated, "I expect you here Monday and Friday mornings. Surely your client can be switched." Mrs. Truman landed notably hard on the word "here."

Marti refused and assumed the interview was over and didn't feel terribly disappointed that she wouldn't be hired by this woman but as she rose to leave Mrs. Truman snapped, "This is very upsetting—but Monday mornings and Friday afternoon then."

Pedaling her way back to her retreat, Marti almost wished she had just turned the Truman woman down. The prospect of having to be in the Truman home twice a week was depressing.

As she pedaled around the Iverson barn her mind was on the unpleasant Truman woman, and on rounding the corner by the office door she nearly collided with a tall man leaning against a support beam; someone enjoying bird and animal life in the rustic back yard, but Marti's reaction was terror and she had leaped from the bike pitching it at the startled man and had whirled to run when she heard the loud, "Whoa! Hey!" and she knew instantly it wasn't Ted.

Shocked and feeling ashamed, Marti rapidly set the bike to rights, mumbling apologies.

But Chris had caught a glimpse of cheeks and lips that had gone chalky white, he'd heard the gasp and could still see in his mind's eye how the bike had been thrown. What in God's name was this woman so afraid of? He didn't move towards her, but raised a quietening hand, saying, "No problem. Sorry I startled you. Is the bike okay?"

Trying to sound normal, and wanting only to get behind her own door, Marti had answered with "Yes—I'm sure it is. I'm so sorry almost running you over." With that she would have vanished up the stairs, but the man had extended a hand and was pleasantly introducing himself. "I'm Chris Losinski" and giving a nod to his office door added, "I was taking a break—that's my shop, by the way."

With no option but to introduce herself in return, she put out her own hand and felt it warmly enclosed in his.

"I'm Marti Gracek. Nice to meet you, Mr. Losinski," she quickly removed her hand as he was saying, "Chris, please. Just Chris," and now she seemed to be melting backwards towards the steps leading up to her apartment while murmuring, "Yes. Thank you. Good-bye." Her rubber-soled shoes made no sounds as she made her escape.

Chris was left wondering what was going on with this woman. Her hand had been shaking badly. She had mistaken him for someone. The husband she had separated from...or *running* from? Chris didn't doubt for a moment that he had just witnessed someone in fear for her life.

Closing her door behind herself, Marti locked it, then sank onto one of the old wooden kitchen chairs and rested her head on her arms. She had mistaken the carpenter from downstairs as Ted. She'd believed for one horrible moment he had tracked her down! And what must Mr. Losinski be thinking of her now? That she was a crazy woman? Maybe she was if other men were beginning to look like Ted. The voice was vastly different: nice, kind—his eyes weren't mean like Ted's. Mr. Los—*Chris* had seemed to care how she felt. There was a goodness present in this man that had come across to her. Marti pulled herself together and turned her attention back to her newest client, Roxann Truman, and then put all the pertinent information about her into the client record book. Working for Mrs. Truman would be neither easy, nor pleasant, but it meant money to live on. She had survived so much worse, so don't complain about one unpleasant woman, Marti told herself.

It wasn't noon yet, but close enough to fix a sandwich and some fruit for her lunch, then trim the grass and weeds from around the barn foundation. It was too nice to stay indoors. She had heard there were great walking trails in Decorah's Phelps Park. A bike ride to see it would be a great way to be out on such a nice afternoon. She would take leftover popcorn to feed to the birds and squirrels.

Marti had trimmed her way around most of the barn foundation on her hands and knees when she heard Gilbert's voice at her side.

"Aren't you the busy one? Looks nice, Marti! Thora says come on in for a cookie and coffee. You wouldn't want to miss out on her raisin-oatmeal cookies, would you?"

Within minutes, Marti was in the Iversons' pleasant kitchen with the bustling couple talking over each other and all enjoying warm cookies fresh from the oven, with a cup of hot coffee in her hand. She had removed her hat, fluffing the short, soft waves of her hair with her fingers, laying the dark glasses, with the hat, on the floor at her feet. And moments later the sound of footsteps was heard in the hallway and Chris's voice came cheerfully, "I smell Thora's raisin cookies!"

It had not occurred to Marti anyone but herself had been invited in for coffee by the affable couple, but now Chris was pulling a chair up beside her, his eyes taking in the wide-eyed pixie face framed in silvery white waves.

Chris was bowled off his feet in a manner of speaking and was momentarily speechless but couldn't miss seeing Marti's discomfort to have him staring at her face.

He was quick to pick up the conversation, eyeing the plate of cookies and making a show of picking the biggest cookie there; and soon talk and laughter was flowing between the charming couple and their two renters of whom they had become so fond.

When asked what her plans were for the rest of the afternoon, Marti made light of it with, "Just a few errands I need to see to—glad it's such a nice day."

Thora had known about the interview with Roxann Truman, and curious to know how that went, asked what Marti thought of the well-heeled woman who was frequently in the society section of the newspaper on various committees. Cautiously, Marti answered she hoped to get to know Mrs. Truman better, but truthfully knew nothing about her as of now. But of the Rasmussons, Marti obviously had great empathy for them and shared with the listeners around the table how stunning Emma's rosemal folk art was, as well as how she admired their blue door and beautiful benches covered in the Rosemalingen; how sad Emma would most likely not be painting again.

Marti wondered how many years had passed since anyone had shown such interest—real interest—in anything she had to say. All three listened, fascinated by the soft, shy voice.

After thirty minutes, Marti excused herself, thanking Thora for the "out-of-this-world" cookies, and then thanked everyone for a pleasant visit. She had popped her hat on her head and left putting the glasses back on. Plus, carrying off several of Thora's cookies in a sandwich baggie.

Thora stared after Marti's retreating figure and at the sound of the front door closing, spoke with puzzlement.

"She is so beautiful. Why is she hiding?" The men were silent. It was only later in the day at the shop, out of Thora's hearing following a moment when the men's conversation had lagged, Gilbert in an almost expressionless voice spoke the words both men inwardly thought.

"He's hunting her. The husband." And slowly, Chris nodded his head, his lips thinning to a tight line, the light gray eyes ice cold. He had no idea how to help Marti.

When Gilbert had left, Chris had busied himself at his desk for some time. He had tried to locate a Frank Gracek in St. Louis and come up with nothing. Lost in thought, he sat at his desk, tapping a pencil lightly on his desk. There was a Martha Gracek Sweltzer in Des Moines. Chris was on a mission.

GULLIVER

It had been an especially nice time in Thora's kitchen and Marti was glad now it had happened. They were all such nice people. Even Chris. At least he seemed that way. So had Ted. At first. You just couldn't really know anyone completely—right? Her thoughts sometimes seemed to run in circles. Pay attention to the traffic before you get yourself run over, she told herself—she was pedaling and trying to read a brochure map to Phelps Park. Trying to do two things at one time with a preoccupied mind in traffic was not a good plan.

The park was well-kept, clean, with an attractive entrance leading into a spacious parking area where Marti spotted a bike rack to chain her bike to. Reaching into the saddle bag she took out the popcorn and the baggie with cookies, and started out on the nearest foot path, taking her time to enjoy all of nature around her, and to listen for the sounds of birds and insects. She especially liked bees and wasn't afraid of them. Leave them alone and they will leave you alone. What industrious workers they were. Marti had once observed a bee that died in the middle of a flower, its feet clinging to the petal with its head and body directed into its center. She had observed it for quite a while in fascination.

Benches were placed conveniently along the neat path with trash bins close by. A squirrel chattered at her to go away, but that was where Marti made use of one of the benches and seated herself taking inventory of any bird activity.

She began tossing a few pieces of the popped corn while watching the squirrel still "barking" at her. A sparrow--bright-eyed, was first to come closest to Marti's offering. In the serenity of the park, undisturbed, Marti was lost in thoughts of her family, her mother. She had called Shirley at her workplace when she knew her friend would be preparing to leave for the day. She had shared the good news of being in comfortable surroundings and was earning enough to sustain herself. She sent her love to her mother and sister through Shirley, re-stressing it would not be possible to see or talk to them until she knew Ted couldn't reach or hurt them. Shirley had related to Marti how her mother had cried terribly during that first contact with her, but to finally learn the truth of Marti's abandonment of them had brought as much relief as it did pain.

Telling her friend to keep up her guard, and to be safe, Marti had said her good-bye knowing it would be a long time before she felt safe enough to call oftener.

Marti sat so still for such a long time that the squirrel had ceased its noise and come down to the popcorn and sitting on its haunches was holding a popped kernel to its mouth with both front paws. Several sparrows hopped and pecked at the offering while a blue jay swooped in and left with a kernel in its beak. Tossing a few more, she opened the baggie and took a cookie out for herself. Nibbling to make the treat last, knowing she should be getting back, she reluctantly reached for the leftover popcorn and saw movement near the ground in overgrowth under a large bush—and froze, feeling goosebumps rise on her arms and neck. Something crept, low to the ground towards some popcorn, and the birds and squirrel vanished. Staring intensely, Marti recognized a dog, emaciated, a chain about its neck. One leg didn't look right. The animal tried to keep off it as it nosed to the popcorn, swallowing the bits lying about. Marti watched it with pity as the creature warily watched her while it ate kernel after kernel. When she tried to coax it to come to her, it had turned and disappeared into the bushes without a sound. Marti dumped the rest of the popcorn in a pile by the bench, placing Thora's cookies beside it; and left feeling depressed.

SENA DAHL

A phone call from a "Sena Dahl," in need of Marti's house-keeping services, that evening helped dispel the depression she had felt after the dog encounter. The time of the interview was for the next morning, a Saturday, as Ms. Dahl was a stenographer at the courthouse on weekdays.

Marti woke to a dark day, wet and chill. The rainslicker would be needed for her to ride to Sena Dahl's home. At her sink, washing up her breakfast dishes, Marti looked again out the window over the sink hoping the weather might be improving, and could hardly believe her eyes to see the thin, limping form of the brown and white dog. How in the world had it been able to follow her back to the barn?

Going through Henry's well-used utensils, Marti found a

battered pan to hold water for the dog, and an old, chipped bowl that she began to fill with whatever she could find to feed the poor thing. Bread, eggs, milk, a hotdog. In the bathroom, she picked up the well-worn rug by the sink and folded it over an arm. Picking up the food and water, Marti made her way down the steps. There was no sign of the dog, but she placed the food and water with little clicks and clangs, calling, "Come! Come on fella." then placed the rug near the barn wall and went back upstairs.

When she went down again to leave for her interview, the food was gone, water was dripped outside the pan, and the rug was rumpled. But no dog. Dropping a slice of bread in the bowl, Marti got on the bike and left for her interview feeling happy. She would buy dog food on her way home.

It may have been a drizzly morning on a gray day, but Ms. Sena Dahl was literally, a ray of sunshine. She swung the door wide at Marti's knock and greeted her with a big smile on an open cheerful face. She led Marti from the entry into a front room in a lot of disorder. Sena started clearing a space for her guest to be seated. A couple small pillows along with a "throw" were tossed behind an over-stuffed chair which in turn caused a hissing, spitting cat to erupt from behind the chair to crouch under the coffee table beside a pile of magazines and a jumble of shoes where it continued to emit long, low growls with a few hisses.

As Marti took a seat on the cleared sofa, a paw with claws extended made a fast swipe at her foot. Marti found herself unable to drag her eyes off the unpleasant creature.

"That's Narci. It's best to leave her alone," came from Sena along with a happy laugh. "Miss Narci Sistic. No one else wanted her." And more laughter followed. The interview was delightful, and there was no doubt Sena was a terrible housekeeper. Not that it bothered or embarrassed her. Marti guessed her to be close in age to herself. An attractive woman who was comfortable with herself, free of pretensions.

Marti looked forward to working in Sena's home but would be keeping a safe distance from nasty Narci! Leaving the untidy, disorganized home brought up an image of the Truman home where not a thing was out of place in the sterile atmosphere. With a mild shock, Marti found a similarity between her own former "home," with all its sand-colored carpeting, and of the woman's home. The few family portraits and pictures of the Trumans' son helped break up the colorless expanses, but it had the same cold atmosphere she had felt in her former "home."

Marti picked up the dog food on her return trip to "her retreat," feeling good about the interview and grateful that two more hours a week had been added to her schedule. Guiding her bike under the shelter of the deck, Marti's eyes went immediately to the food bowl, and a smile came at the sight of the empty bowl.

She hadn't heard the office door open behind her but turned quickly at Chris's voice.

"Looks like you are a dog owner, Marti. How did that come about?"

Her smile had stayed as she answered, "I'm not really sure, but it's a sure thing he needs to be cared about!"

Chris hadn't answered but his unspoken thought was "Don't we all," as he watched the happy smile that hadn't left her face. She had then told him how the dog had followed her, somehow, from Phelps Park.

Marti's reputation as an exceptional housekeeper brought her a fourth job that wasn't in a home. She was hired after the bank closed to vacuum and clean floors, breakroom, and restroom. She was let in by a night guard. It was her best paying job, and she never felt uncomfortable being alone in the empty building.

Days followed days that became weeks, and those in turn

became months as Marti slowly forged a life for herself, keeping a distance from others for their protection. And to protect her own heart.

To come home to the plain and simple barn where a damaged canine waited for her return was balm to Marti's soul. It took time, but the first time Gulliver let her touch him had made her cry. She had named him after Gulliver's Travels as she wondered where he had come from, where he had been, how he had found his way to her. Hungry, tired, all but at the end of his strength. And finally, Gully let Marti carefully unhook the heavy chain from around his neck. He'd licked her hand, looking steadily at her eyes. He hadn't wanted to come into the apartment, but with winter's arrival, curling up on the rug outside the door became too miserable and he limped inside as Marti held the door wide and coaxed. When Marti wasn't at one of her jobs, the two were inseparable. No one but Marti could touch Gully, though it was men especially he did not like.

Seated on Henry's beat-up sofa with an old blanket draped over her shoulders and Gully leaning against her, Marti was thinking back over her day as her fingers absently stroked a velvety ear of the dozing dog. It was Tuesday, Sena's day for housecleaning. Marti had enjoyed putting the delightfully funny woman's living quarters into attractive order. Sena didn't care if Marti moved the furniture around, or rearranged things, and the little duplex had taken on a whole new look. The sink was always full of dirty dishes and laundry lay piled in a heap when she arrived on Tuesdays. Marti had taken it all over, even to the laundering of the bed linen. Today, in removing the bedding, a man's single black sock had turned up in the sheets.

Marti had laughed and laughed! The Friday afternoon prior, Marti had emptied a small waste basket beneath the sink in Roxann Truman's master bathroom and had found a man's single black sock. She had wondered why such a smart, fun, attractive woman as Sena appeared to have no social life. Marti hoped things worked out well for her. When it came to Roxann, she thought her to be a vain, shallow, self-centered woman. "And controlling," she added in her mind. Apparently, Roxann and Miss Narci Sistic were like "sisters" under the skin. Marti was careful not to engage with either one.

The Truman home was never out of order, and Marti's work went fast, as it had in the home she had shared with Ted. He at least was out of the house as she did her work there, but at the Trumans, Roxann followed her every move, unpleasantly giving orders as if she were either stupid or would filtch something if not under constant surveillance. Unpleasant, yes! But Marti reminded herself it put bread on the table for herself and Gully, as well as keeping a roof over their heads.

When it became impossible to navigate the ice and snow on the bicycle, Chris had insisted on driving her to work and picking her up. He had been offended when Marti tried to pay him. She treated him as a good friend, but suspected he felt differently about her. She didn't want to think about what Ted might do to anyone she cared about if he caught up to her, and so kept the barrier's up, discouraging any closeness.

Marti was content in the simple life she had fashioned, praying in her heart to be left in peace. Two things had come about that filled her with deep gratitude. The first had been the violin. And then, Gully.

Soon after Marti's move into the Iversons' barn loft, Gilbert had tuned up his violin one evening and begun playing the beautiful classics he loved. The perfect, soaring notes had come to Marti's ears as she sat in the fading daylight on the balcony deck mesmerizing her with its beauty. Unable to put the music out of her mind she had gone to the Iverson home several days later and remarked on the music. Gilbert was flattered, and brought the violin out to show her, and demonstrated a few melodies on it. Observing the genuine awe and longing in her face as she had listened, he told her he was a retired high school music teacher, asking if she played any instruments in school, and she had nodded. "I had piano lessons when I was in grade school. In high school I played flute in the band."

Gilbert had asked her if she was interested in learning the violin and there had been a silence before her soft voice had stated simply, "I can't afford the instrument, or lessons." As she had left, she looked at Gilbert saying she hoped she'd be lucky enough to hear him play again.

When Marti's rent had come due, she'd tapped on Thora's kitchen door window with money in hand, and Thora's cheerful voice had called for her to walk in. It seemed the Iversons' house always smelled of such mouth-watering aromas, and that day had been no different. A large pan of caramel pecan rolls was on the counter and Thora was drizzling glaze over the tops. Within minutes, Marti was seated at the table, her mouth full of warm pecan sweet roll. Gilbert had strolled in, depositing a bundle on the floor near the door before joining the women at the table for his share of the bounty.

With the consumption of the fresh bakery complete, Gilbert turned his cherubic countenance towards Marti, looking very much pleased with himself. As he opened his mouth to speak, his beaming wife snatched the conversation, saying, "Gilbert has finally begun sorting through his collection of stuff and—" There Gilbert took attention back to himself with, "dug out an old, but good—" Holding up a hand to his wife, the elderly man had finished with, "—violin!" And they had both beamed with delight. The bundle by the door had then been unwrapped and placed in Marti's hands. She couldn't stop shaking her head in disbelief, awe on her face.

Gilbert had then offered free lessons if she chose to accept his offer. And right there he had given Marti her first lesson from an old, yellowed book; sending her back, walking on air, to her apartment with a first lesson assignment. She proved to be the ideal student, practicing diligently to master the technique Gilbert did with ease.

The only one to show disapproval of the violin practice in those early days was Gully who begged at the door to go out. When the weather became too cold, he hid under Marti's bed.

But the days came when he no longer tried to escape.

SPRING

Chris had given up asking Marti to movies, or a dinner out. She was always kind in her refusals, and immovable, but there seemed a pervasive sadness there, too. He felt in some way he mattered to her. He had recently invited her to his church and her reaction still puzzled him. He could only describe what he saw as being repelled by the invitation, which she covered up with quick excuses.

What in the world had happened to her that she should practically cloister herself? To find out he needed to follow-up on the name "Sweltzer." Martha Gracek Sweltzer who was located in Des Moines.

Time to take a little trip. Chris packed several changes of clothes in a duffel bag, gassed up his car, locked his shop with a "Back in Three Days" sign with the return date and stuck it in the door window; then popped his head in at the Iversons just long enough to say, "Good-bye" and when he'd be back. The roly-poly couple were left speechless, immobile and befuddled.

As Chris covered the miles to Des Moines, he tried to work up different scenarios for why he needed information on a Martha (or Marti?) Gracek. Nothing fit together well at all. He decided to make it up as he went.

Once in Des Moines, he looked for a room well into the city in hope he would be close to whatever he'd be looking for. At the check-in desk he asked the receptionist where the city library was located, hoping it would be close. It wasn't. In the phone book in his room, he found Sweltzer Real Estate and Insurance Agency along with the address. At least that was a little closer. He headed directly for the city library and requested to see the micro-film of newspapers from two-and-a-half to three years earlier. Seated in a dark alcove alone, except for one other person--a man hunched over, studying micro-film records just as Chris was about to be also.

Over an hour passed and with eyes burning, neck and shoulders aching, Chris was sure he had found Marti's past.

The picture almost fooled him. It was black and white, but the long haired, dark-eyed woman's face had Marti's features. The hair was described as red, the eyes brown, but Chris knew it was Marti, described as missing. The police had been in-volved after a failed kidnapping on the woman, and during a follow-up visit to her home had discovered her not only miss-ing from the residence, but the husband insisted his wife had run off with another man after the pair had emptied his safe as well. There was damage where the money was kept, and all the wife's personal effects were gone. Nothing could be proved or disproved.

Chris jotted down the address of Marti's former home and closed the notepad. He didn't believe she had run off with another man. But the missing money? None of this fit the Marti Chris knew.

He was troubled and tired but satisfied to have what information he had been able to glean from the micro-film. Now he wanted to get a look at Ted Sweltzer, learn something about him. Chris had looked the man up in the phone book and now knew that address as well as the workplace. Apparently, Ted had moved from the home he'd had with Marti. Now Chris had three places he wanted to check out.

It hadn't been the best night's rest Chris had ever had, but he felt surprisingly ready in the morning to get started on the search for Marti's past. He wanted to see where she had lived; and, if he were lucky, talk with any neighbors who might have known her. He'd decided early morning might work best if he wanted to catch people at home before getting out shopping or visiting. Twenty-some minutes had passed before he pulled up to the curb in front of a large, white two-story house with attached garage. Chris doubted much would be garnered from new owners of the home. A dog barked somewhere in the house when he rang the doorbell. A woman answered the door with her fingers hooked in the collar of a golden Labrador. Chris introduced himself with the explanation that he was doing research on the disappearance of a Martha Sweltzer from this residence three years earlier. When she asked if he was the police, he improvised, saying, "No. Her family wants to find her. Would you mind if I ask a few questions?"

She began shaking her head, saying, "I wasn't here then. I know nothing."

Chris had answered, "I realize that. But when you looked at the home with the thought to buy, what was your impression of the home? Anything seem odd to you?" He'd watched the woman's face closely as she frowned, concentrating on memories from three years earlier. He remained quiet, intent.

"Well--," came out slowly, thoughtfully, "I will tell you none of my neighbors had anything nice to say about the husband.

I met him and never would have guessed that his neighbors thought him to be abusive to his wife." A moment later, the woman added that she and her husband discussed what they had heard about the previous owners when their dog had dug up bones in the backyard, that turned out to be dog bones; yet according to neighbors the Sweltzers had never had any pets.

Thanking her for her assistance, Chris gave the woman a business card from his hotel, with his own name written on the back, asking her to call and leave a message if she recalled anything that might help find the missing woman.

He had returned to his car, and gotten in, but had been sitting behind the wheel, lost in thought for several minutes, his eyes roaming neighborhood yards. Across the street, almost out of sight, Chris saw a woman on a kneeling pad, half hidden by a flowering bush she was "feeding," or fertilizing, and in moments he was out of the car and heading across the street.

It was obvious Chris had startled the intent gardener. He apologized sincerely, and again introduced himself, and used the same story on this woman, too.

A sadness settled over her face when he mentioned Martha's family was searching for her. Her concerned eyes were watery as she told of hearing the screams, and cries of "Please, stop" that carried out of the house on several occasions.

Chris's shock didn't show on his face, but it hit like a rock in the pit of his stomach. He had been right. Marti had run for her life. But why had she not involved the police? Why had no one intervened? It seemed several people knew and did nothing.

Back in the car, Chris looked up the Sweltzer's Realty & Insurance business address and set off to have a look at a man he already knew he despised, and also knowing he could not allow his feelings to be known by Ted Sweltzer.

Pulling into a parking space at Sweltzer's business, Chris had formed a suitable explanation for his stop at the realtor's office. As he entered the reception area, an attractive young woman at the desk looked up and flashed a brilliant white smile. He nodded to her and casually looked about the room, then walked to a display of brochures on homes for sale and began thumbing through them, finally pulling one out to more closely examine.

He was aware someone was approaching before a man's voice pleasantly inquired if he could be of any help.

Turning, Chris knew he was facing the man who was the terror of Marti. It took all of his restraint to keep a blank face as he assessed this man who exuded friendliness and charm. He was almost as tall as Chris. Tanned, well-groomed, expensively dressed, handsome. This was a man who turned the heads of women. A man with a perfect smile that didn't reach his eyes. Chris went into his story of picking up brochures on houses his wife could look at when he was back home. They were looking to move to Des Moines and opening his own carpentry business. The wife was near-term with their second child. They wanted a good school nearby for their five-year-old.

Ted responded by picking out several brochures for Chris with reassurance something new came in regularly and finding exactly what they wanted would be no problem. When Chris had asked if Ted had kids in school, he had shaken his head and said, "No. That hasn't been in the cards," and moved the conversation back to houses Chris should consider when he and his wife could come in together. Chris noted the young receptionist's starry-eyed gaze fastened on her employer.

From the hotel phonebook, Chris had found Sweltzers home address and...out of curiosity, had driven past the residence on his return to the hotel, noting it as a small rental unit, attractively maintained.

Thoughtfully going over all that he had learned about Marti, he knew it was not nearly enough to help her in any way. He thought about talking to someone in the police department but was troubled that Marti had run after the failed kidnapping—the police were already involved. But still, she had run. Why? He began to plan how to have a conversation with her and get everything out in the open. He would do all in his power to help and protect her.

He would be on his way tomorrow. He pulled in and parked under a streetlight and walked into the hotel lobby. The clerk looked up as he passed and called out, "Mr. Losinski, message for you." Plucking a folded note from a slot with Chris's room number over it, he had handed it to him. Too curious to wait, he flipped it open, looking at the signature first and recalled the gardening lady. He had given her a card with his name on it just as he had to the dog owner. As he read the note, he knew he had another stop to make.

The kind-hearted gardener had gone out of her way—perhaps out of regret for not helping Marti? —and contacted a friend who had told her, at the time the "kidnapping thing" was in the newspaper; she had seen Marti in the beauty shop with a bruised face. It was called "Katie's Kuts & Kurls."

Chris had showered, shaved, and dressed earlier than he liked but he had been unable to sleep longer. It had been a restless night. He had a leisurely breakfast in the hotel dining room and enjoyed a second cup of coffee as he read the morning paper, dawdling till the hands on a wall clock indicated if he left the hotel now, he would reach "Katie's Kuts & Kurls" by nine a.m.

The beauty shop was open with two clients there, waiting to be called by their hairdressers. Chris could see three beauticians each setting up her own station among six stalls. The eyes of all the women turned towards Chris as he approached the manager standing over the appointments book.

Never had he ever felt so out of place as he did now. Reaching the desk with the manager staring at him over the glasses perched near the tip of her nose, he had hardly begun with "Hi, I'm Chris Losinski and I'm looking for a missing woman, Martha Gracek Sw—" when the crash of scissors hitting the tile floor drew everyone's eyes to the curvy woman at the closest station who had overheard Chris. He had no doubt whatsoever he was looking at Marti's hairdresser. Continuing with "Sweltzer," he finished with, "Her family is desperate to find her." Taking more hotel cards with his name on the back out of a jacket pocket, he gave one each to the manager and the three stylists standing so still and listening. Thanking them, he finished with, "Anything you might remember, please let me know." And he had lingered just a little at the first station, looking directly into wide, frightened eyes, and whispered, "For Marti," as a shaky hand had taken the card. He was shocked that even Marti's former hairdresser still feared Ted three years later.

Back in his car, Chris could only sit, unable to assimilate how evil some men were; claiming to love a woman, would permanently scar her body, then mentally and emotionally destroy her. Even kill her. There had to be a special place in hell for men like Ted.

Chris had made himself comfortable in the lobby, prepared for a long wait. It was a little after six-thirty p.m. when the beautician walked in and Chris breathed a sigh of thanks to God. He had felt so strongly she would meet with him, but another part of his mind told him he was a fool. Now he put a hand out to her and gripped the warm hand that met his. So intent on her, Chris completely missed seeing a big man amble into the lobby, then settle himself comfortably behind artificial plants.

"When you called her "Marti" I knew I could trust you, Mr. Losinski. What are we going to do to keep her safe? I'm Shirley Hebner, by the way." Chris could have hugged her. Fortunately, he did not.

The hotel dining room made a good place to meet where they found a quiet, more private corner; and over coffee, in low tones, Shirley started to tell what she knew. And again, Chris missed seeing the big fellow from the lobby make his way to a distant table out of Chris's line of vision.

Shirley began telling Chris all Marti had revealed to her that first night, keeping her emotions under tight control as she watched the reality of Marti's life cause Chris's head to sink until it rested heavily in his hands. Chris didn't speak for several minutes after Shirley finished. The words she heard gave her chills.

"I will kill him."

"Shhhh! Don't even say such a thing, Chris! He will be dealt with. If not in this life, it will be in the next! But I believe there is nothing that man is not capable of. Marti knew about his last woman, an Audra O'Neil, a wealthy socialite who dumped him when Marti disappeared, and the police were involved because of that odd, attempted kidnapping. That woman died in a fall off her balcony on New Year's Eve, and I believe he caused her death. She'd had several drinks at a party, and the fall happened after going home at four a.m. Police suspected something but could prove nothing.

Chris couldn't take his eyes from the face of this wholesome, decent, empathic woman. What she was saying sounded unbelievable. But the emptiness in Ted's eyes came back to him as he recalled the warm, pleasant talk of finding exactly what Chris and his wife were looking for in a future home in Des Moines. He believed Shirley.

As their meeting drew to an end, they had each other's phone numbers, and Chris now knew where Marti's mother lived, her last name since re-marrying, and her phone.

Then as they rose from their seats, ready to say good-bye, Shirley had smiled widely, then laughed, saying, "I'd like you to meet someone," and when she looked past Chris he had turned to look also and saw a bear of a man coming towards him with a big smile, and he realized Shirley's husband had accompanied her to this meeting with a stranger. Of course.

Back in his room, he struggled again over trying to have a "clearing-the-air" talk with Marti. Would she be angry he had found Ted, found Shirley, and was now thinking of visiting her parents? In for a dime, in for a dollar—Chris decided he might as well add meeting her family to the act of finding Shirley and Ted. He began planning a road trip to Rochester, Minnesota.

ARCHIE REID

As Chris had been uncovering details of Marti's past life in Des Moines, fate was intervening in her life in Decorah.

It had been an untroubled three years for Marti in the dignified college town of Decorah. She had enough work to sustain herself. She was content, and Gully was perfect company for her. She reminded herself frequently to keep her guard up—Ted would not be forgetting anything, or anyone who crossed him, or cost him. And Marti knew she had crossed both lines.

For all her caution, in spite of keeping distance from others, of hiding behind a brimmed cap and dark glasses, she could have no control over coincidence. The simple act of going for her usual grocery shopping, in the usual store, in her usual attire, she walked past a car with a man waiting in it for his wife and mother-in-law, in the grocery parking lot—and that changed everything.

Marti's attention was on the sacks in her hands and keeping her head tipped so the wind didn't take her hat, and she didn't see the Des Moines license plate, or the intense stare by the man, at what showed of her face as she tilted her head in his direction. He was a police officer, trained to be observant. And Archie Reid had met Marti a few times at different functions which Ted and his wife attended.

"I'll be damned. Wait till Ted hears this!" drummed in his head. He needed to follow her, see where she went. His wife and her mother were inside getting the old lady stocked up before heading home themselves. He hated these boring trips to see the old bat—he knew she couldn't stand him, but the infrequent trips shut the "ol' ball-n-chain" up for a while. They hadn't been in the store long. Surely Martha lived nearby to be carrying her shopping. He could be right back. So what if they had to wait a few minutes.

He turned the key in the ignition and slowly eased out of his parking space and began the cautious tailing of Marti who had unchained a bike and put the sacks into the bike saddle bags. He knew how to remain unnoticed, but he hoped she wasn't going far. Sure enough, she turned, into a quiet neighborhood and up the drive to a neat house set back amongst big trees, by an old barn. Archie was now in possession of the street name and home address and was back in time to see his wife and mother-in-law just coming out of the grocery store. He was filled with excitement over his big discovery and called Ted from his mother-in-law's phone as the women put away groceries. Ted answered the phone as Chris drove out of the Sweltzer parking lot.

By the time Chris and Shirley were meeting in the hotel dining room, Ted was almost to Decorah unaware Marti would be busy until late with her work at the bank.

After meeting with Shirley, Chris called the Iversons to say he would be gone another day, leaving them more confused than before.

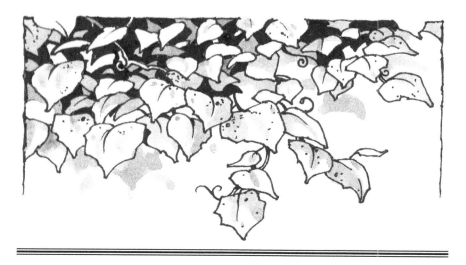

JOB 15:16

"...one who is detestable and corrupt: A person who drinks malice like water."

When Archie put his call through to Ted it was a moment that re-ignited his need for revenge on Martha. Over the three-year span of Martha's flight, Ted had searched on his own and could find no trace of where Martha could have gone. He had tried to locate her mother without success; he had gone after her hairdresser; and finally, had hired a private investigator. The man had explored several methods to track missing persons before informing Ted some people manage "to go to earth and not be found." Or they died. What Ted didn't know was the man he had hired wanted no part in putting Ted on anyone's trail. He had a gut instinct of what Ted had in mind for his missing wife, and he hoped no other P.I. would be hired.

But Archie was a similar form of Ted and he had no compunction whatsoever over Ted's woman "learning her place." He had been delighted to give Ted the news of what he had stumbled on.

Ted listened to Archie's news with no interruptions, slowly feeling a sense of impending justification for himself. How he had waited for, hoped for, what Archie had stumbled on with no effort. Martha would soon get what she so richly deserved. Just as Audra had. With that memory slipping in, Ted slowly leaned back relaxed in his chair. It had been over two-and-a-half years since he had given up on convincing Audra he had nothing to do with his wife's disappearance. He had played the part of the wronged husband to perfection. He had pleaded, placated, gifted, and doted on Audra; flawlessly, as Ted saw it, only to have her grow more cold towards him each day until she had, finally, very bluntly told him to stay away from her. To not call her again. He had blamed her friends as turning her against him; he had been well aware he was not liked by Audra's three best friends. It had taken patience and coordinated planning to have his revenge. If he couldn't enjoy the luxury life with Audra, then she would not enjoy her luxurious life either. He had made his plans methodically when he heard of the big New Year Costume Ball Audra and her crowd were having in the ballroom of the elegant hotel where Audra lived in her deceased father's penthouse. She had inherited everything after her father disinherited his alcoholic, drug-addicted son. Ted had gone to the best costumers in the city to check out disguises for his New Year's Eve schemes. One that included gloves and mask. And he already knew his way around the hotel. In his disguise, he had easily "waltzed" his way to the ballroom to be sure Audra was with her friends and left--he had the key to the penthouse, and he remembered the penthouse elevator code.

It was a long wait in Audra's "home", and he acquainted himself well with her property. He had heard her unlock her door, and then the voice of another woman, and Ted had hidden himself deep in a guest room closet which he had scouted out earlier to be on the safe side. He knew the visitor's voice but wasn't sure of the name. Audra's best friend—Patrice? He heard the low murmur of their voices, the clink of ice and crystal, laughter. He settled down to wait. A half-hour passed, at least. He changed his position as best he could. When voices sounded closer, more clear, he tensed until he heard, "No—I'd love to—got to get home to the kiddies. Call me later, okay?" and Ted relaxed at the sound of the door closing. He let several minutes pass, relishing the moment.

Knowing there was no one to hear, he had let her scream a few times after he had come up behind her and put a choke hold across her throat with his arm. He had squeezed until she passed out, then quickly removed the beautiful ruby and diamond ring she never took off. It was the last birthday gift her father had given her before his unexpected death a few years earlier. Ted pushed it up to the middle of the little finger of his left hand. Audra was coming around again. Ted punched her, slamming her head onto the floor. He would have preferred having her conscious, and aware of going over the balcony, but he didn't want screams attracting anyone before he could be well on his way. He had unlocked the penthouse double glass doors to the outside sitting area and had set a wine-filled goblet on the protective barrier. Going back in he gathered Audra up, draping her over his shoulder. He then positioned her as though sitting on the balcony ledge, and shoved her backwards. He watched as the limp, silent form plummeted to the concrete earth. Then, knocking over the wine glass, he took one more quick look about; and whistling a jaunty tune, he had let himself out, locking the door behind, leaving by the stairs.

Ted liked thinking about that night. He liked settling scores. Reaching to the back of his business desk drawer, he withdrew an ivory keepsake box that required a code to be opened—a gift from Audra in better times. He pressed in the code and, taking out the ring, he slipped it on his left pinky as far as it would go. Now it was time to settle up with Martha.

Ted notified his secretary/receptionist to say he wasn't feeling well and was heading home. Adding he would be in touch with her. Once in his apartment, he had dressed "down" in darker clothing and filled an overnight bag, planning a very fast trip to, and from, Decorah.

On arrival in what he thought of as a "nothing place," he checked into a cheap motel on the edge of the town and waited for darkness. While it had still been light, he had checked out the neat house set back in the yard, with the big sheltering trees. It would be easy, he thought. Nice and private as soon as it was dark.

Parking a short distance from the address supplied by Archie, Ted had walked casually to where he could cut across the back yard towards the lighted windows of the house. He'd paid no attention to the barn. In the shelter of the darkness made deeper by trees and foliage, he looked into the lighted rooms, only to see an old man and his wife. Ted had watched as the old woman washed and put away dishes. He watched that light go out, and he moved to where the old couple sat watching the television. By ten-thirty the pair had turned off the TV and left that room in darkness. It was obvious they were turning in for the night. And Martha was nowhere to be seen.

Ted was beyond furious, and he mentally cursed Archie most foully as he made his way back through the trees in the direction he'd come, only this time at the back of the barn he noticed the stairs for the first time. He could see they led to an upper deck and silently he mounted them to a locked door. Windows were on each side, but only darkness within. It seemed to be an apartment. It made sense—Martha could no doubt afford only a cheap apartment. Apparently, she was out for the evening, the slut! He would have noticed lights when he cut through earlier, had there been any. Ted silently set to work opening Martha's locked door and didn't hear the near-silent guttural snarl deep in Gully's throat. He wasn't a barker. He'd painfully learned not to bark long before he'd met Marti. Now he "three-legged-stepped" to the door as it opened and awkwardly, he lunged, sinking fangs into an arm.

Ted screamed, and flung himself back and away from the doorway, dropping his lock picking tool.

Racing for the steps--a snarling Gully at his heels, Ted wasn't fast enough and the dog bit at him again, catching Ted's pantleg. Ted hit the top stair rail full force on his rib cage; and screaming, he fell tumbling and rolling down the length of the stairs.

In agony he got himself to his feet and took a staggering course through trees and brush to the safety of his car. He made it back to his motel filled with as much rage as pain. No one had been around to question his bloody dishevelment, and he wasted no time getting into his room.

Cleaning the dog bite to his arm with soap, he tore up an undershirt to wrap it. The punctures hadn't bled much, but he had twisted a knee and sprained an ankle, both of which were swelling and painful, but nothing hurt so much as his ribs. It hurt like hell with every breath, with any movement. He need-ed to get back to Des Moines to his doctor as soon as possible. It would be weeks before Ted would be recovered enough to take up the search for Martha. But catch her, he would.

Thora and Gilbert had heard Ted's screams, but by the time the elderly couple was up from their bed, robed and call-ing the police, Ted was almost to his car. And by the time the police arrived he was gone.

Two police officers with high-powered flashlights exam-ined the steps, deck, and on into Marti's apartment. A scrap of dark fabric lay just outside the open door; and it looked as if the burglar had fallen and maybe injured himself. Gully was nowhere to be found. Gilbert reassured the officers the shy dog was no danger to anyone, having lost the use of one leg. And he never barked. The burglar could have panicked meeting a fair-sized dog on opening the door.

At eleven-thirty p.m. Marti arrived by taxi from her job at the bank to find the Iversons and two policemen in her apartment. Sitting white-faced, in shock on the old sofa, she denied knowing of anyone who would want to hurt her and was unaware of the odd expression that crossed Gilbert's face. No one had noticed, and the old man remained silent.

But Marti did know. She had no doubts that Ted had found her. But Gully—had Ted done something to Gully? She wished everyone would just leave.

But the officers were thorough, trying to miss nothing; and found evidence of trampled plants outside the Iversons' windows where someone had been loitering. They would be back in the morning to go over everything again. The old couple had been distraught by all that had happened, but that last bit of information had caused Thora to burst into tears that Gilbert couldn't hug or pat or soothe away. That night no one slept. And before dawn, without a word, Marti was gone.

The police returned early the next day to resume looking over the whole scene and found the door to Marti's apartment propped open, but neither Marti nor her dog could be found. A note was tucked between the door and frame of Chris's office which one of the officers removed and read out loud. "Take care of Gully. Please." That was all. But that Marti had left the way she did, the police believed she did indeed know who had broken into her residence. They also believed whoever it was had first looked for her in the Iverson home. The police by now also surmised Marti had reasons for fearing violence from her pursuer. In questioning Gilbert, who had been reluctant to say much until Chris could be present, the police did learn of the possibility of an abusive husband. They wanted Chris to contact them on his return. And no, Gilbert did not know where he had gone.

Chris returned to his own residence late the next day and could hear his phone ringing as he unlocked his door. As tired as he was, he almost opted to let it ring. When he heard Gilbert's agitated voice on the other end of the line, he was glad he had picked up.

In minutes, Chris was back in his car and breaking a few speed limits on his way to Gilbert and Thora's. The couple were standing under the sign on the barn front. They looked tired as well as stressed, but so glad to see him as he pulled into the small park area. Thora's eyes were red and puffy, but she had apparently cried herself out.

"I want to see her apartment. Tell me everything when we get up there. Is Gully okay? Chris's long legs were covering ground faster than the roly-poly couple could keep up with; and he took the steps two-at-a-time.

"The police want you to come in to answer some questions, Chris." Gilbert sounded a little breathless, and Thora finished with, "Right away, they said."

Chris had entered Marti's residence and now stood looking slowly about her kitchen and living room. There was a clean smell to the rooms, and an orderliness throughout. Henry's old worn second-hand furniture and floor had been scrubbed, cleaned, waxed, oiled. Cared for. On the kitchen table, carefully wrapped, lay Gilbert's old violin. An old blanket lay on the sofa for Gully, his food and water bowl were on the floor by the table. They were empty.

"We propped the door open like Marti did and left food for Gully last night. He must be all right, the bowl is empty—unless something else got to it," Gilbert volunteered hopefully as Thora finished with, "But we haven't seen hide nor hair of him."

The old man fumbled around in a pocket finally bringing out Marti's note and handed it to Chris who read it without speaking, then folded it, putting it inside a jacket pocket.

Stepping into the bedroom, Chris again took in everything about the small room. A neatly made single bed, and old chest of drawers. Marti was a minimalist about her clothing. So little was there, but all was clean, neatly folded or hung up. As though she meant to stay only a short while. What had she taken? Maybe an extra change of clothes?

Gilbert told him of the one small pull-case she had with her when she first had come to his door. A search was done but no such carry-all turned up. Marti was on the run again.

And Chris felt almost physically sick to have gone on the trip to Rochester to see her mother when he should have been here. Now he pinned his hopes on Shirley getting a call from Marti, but he knew she would not expose the ones she loved to the rot of Ted.

Standing on the deck, in the late afternoon sun, Chris studied the trees and thick foliage all around the barn and yard. He looked for the slightest movement. Seating himself on the top step he quietly called the dog's name several times, injecting a whistle, but nothing moved.

Finally, he stood up and turning to Gilbert who'd been quietly watching with Thora, asked permission to put a dog flap entrance on Marti's door.

"Of course," "Yes," "Absolutely," became a chorus from the two oldsters.

"Do you mind if I "camp" here a few nights? I'll hunt up a cot or something to put in the office."

"Chris, it would relieve our minds just knowing you were here. Isn't there a fold-up cot in the house, Thora?"

"Yes! There is! We'll bring the fold-up right over, won't we Gil?" Evening was on the way and having something to do seemed to calm the distracted Iversons. As they hurried off, Chris unlocked his office door, and gathered what was needed to make an access entrance for Gully into Marti's apartment.

He worked on the project all evening and would have forgotten to eat if his landlords hadn't appeared in his shop carrying a picnic basket with food for all three of them. They had again placed food and water at the foot of the stairs for Marti's dog. The food was untouched when the couple said their "good-nights" to Chris and took their weary bodies to bed, where they sent up prayers for Marti, before falling fast asleep.

By the time Chris carried the door up the stairs, the bowl was empty, and he breathed a sigh of relief. In his office, Thora had made up a quite comfortable cot for him; and he had earlier put a call through to the police who would be expecting him in the morning. He was tired and needed sleep, but it took an exceedingly long time before the peace of oblivion came. He hadn't been able to shut out his fears for Marti. Was she okay? Was she somewhere safe? If only she would call him. She'd be worrying about Gully—surely, she'll call.

But she didn't. She wouldn't. She was trying to protect those she loved.

Chris walked into police headquarters by ten a.m. the next day still thinking of his conversation with Shirley. It had been a tough decision for both, but Shirley especially had good reason to fear Ted once he learned she had been to the police headquarters and revealed all she knew of Marti and Ted, as Chris did the same in Decorah. Somehow, maybe, with so much of Ted's secrets exposed the law could be brought into the picture and Marti would be safer. Short of killing the man, Chris knew of no other option.

It was with sinking expectations Chris watched the reaction of the two officers within the interview room as he gave them all he knew about the abuse and flight of Marti three years earlier. Their interest picked up hearing Shirley Hebner was also talking to the police in Des Moines, but regretfully told Chris that until someone did something, or something happened, they could do nothing.

Chris asked about the scrap of fabric found at the scene of the break-in that he believed led back to Ted Sweltzer and was told they could give the evidence to the Des Moines authorities but by now Ted would have disposed of the trousers.

Chris left discouraged.

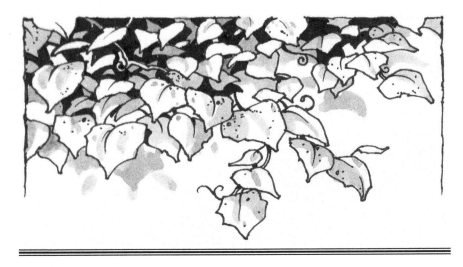

SHIRLEY

Shirley's interview was better due to the fact one of the men taking her report was Tate Osbourn—and he had not forgotten Marti, even after three years. Osbourn didn't show the shock he felt as Shirley told him all that had happened to Marti for sixteen years. She told of Marti hiding in her church belfry before reaching out to her hairdresser, desperate for help, afraid of the police—her husband's friends. The depths to which some men could sink never failed to astound, disgust, and infuriate Osbourn. Ted Sweltzer needed to be put where he could harm no one ever again.

Shirley left the interview unsure if she had been useful or was it of no purpose at all to involve the police, but something Officer Osbourn said told her it had been worthwhile. She had heard him say in a low voice as he left with his assistant, "I knew Martha Sweltzer wanted to tell me something! Oh! —tell Reid I want to see him. Now!"

Shirley's interview was over and several minutes after she left Joe was back, rubbing the back of one hand across his mouth, a sure bet he was wiping a grin off his face. "What's so funny, Joe?"

"What?!—uhh. Uh, nothing. But, uh—sorry to have to inform you, Archie won't be in today. Or tomorrow. Seems the poor bastard broke an ankle." Once again, the back of a hand passed over the twitching lips. It was common knowledge Archie wasn't the best- liked member of the squad.

Tate sat back in his chair, beginning a little rocking motion, and laced his fingers at the back of his neck. "You don't say. Feel free to enlighten me." Joe was beginning to enjoy himself, taking his time coming close to Tate's desk, and drawling,

"We-ell-lll..."

"Spit it out, Joe."

"Archie has a compound fracture of his left ankle. Landed on a curb wrong while chasing two teens on a beer run. Damn shame," Joe finished insincerely.

"And the perps?" prompted Osbourn.

"Nope. But the liquor store has film. So. Matter of time. Do we have to take up a collection for Reid?"

"Yes." Tate tucked his head to hide a grin, and Joe left, glum. The Sweltzer papers, the old and the new, were spread in front of the detective, and he was troubled. What police buddies had Sweltzer connected up with? He couldn't forget Martha Sweltzer's desperate eyes. Or the failed abduction. At least now he knew the woman was alive and well. She had friends. But why had Shirley Hebner mentioned Audra O'Neil's accidental death? Something wasn't passing the smell test.

ON THE RUN

Ted had managed to drive himself back to his residence in terrible pain. There was no choice but to clean himself up and get into something decent, all the while putting together an explanation for his injuries. His story would be to tell his doctor he fell down the basement stairs of one of the unoccupied houses for sale. He'd make up excuses for not coming right in—he could say he'd hoped it wasn't as bad as what it seems now. The bite punctures he would cover with large band aids.

Ted did smooth talk his way around his doctors concerning the broken ribs and sprains but would have to spend time recuperating in his small rental. Having time on his hands and Martha on his mind was not a good combination. All his pain was then laid at her feet along with other imputed *sins*.

He had gotten nowhere on his own search for Martha. The P.I. had been worthless, and he had gotten nothing from the beautician. As he mended, and each day was less painful, Ted felt good enough to do some investigating on his own again. He had remembered the old photo album Martha had kept in her bedside table and was glad now that he hadn't destroyed it. But the night table was in a storage rental unit which he hadn't bothered going through.

He had begun going in to his office for half-days, three days a week, doing paperwork and delegating assignments to the sales personnel. The time had come finally when he decided to go through the storage unit. He'd picked the day for the trip only to have Fate intervene in the form of Officer Osbourn who happened to choose one of Ted's recovery days at home, to drop into his office where the officer learned of the bad fall Ted had taken down the stairs of a house for sale he was inspecting.

"How very interesting," had been Osbourn's thought. He had heard from the Decorah police authorities of an attempted burglary at Marti's apartment. Apparently, her dog had scared him off. Slight damage to the railing near the top of the stairs to the apartment could mean the intruder had fallen. Running from the dog? Osbourn also knew now that Martha— Marti was again on the run which re-affirmed all the more in his mind she knew who had broken into her apartment.

The more Osbourn learned of Ted, the more convinced he became this was a man dangerous to women who crossed him.

Following the news of Ted's injuries, Osbourn headed for the hospital and located the E.R. doctor who had ordered x-rays of Ted's injuries and taped his ribs. He verified the injury was consistent with a fall on stairs. The patient had sprained an ankle, injured a knee, suffered some deep scrapes, bruising; and had covered one wrist with a large band aid, which he declined to have re-dressed. The patient had called it "nothing," but the area looked inflamed. E.R. had been non-stop at the time so the doctor let it go. Antibiotics had been prescribed for the deep scratches anyway.

The name mentioned by Shirley Hebner, Audra O'Neil, was forefront in Osbourn's head as he rang Ted's doorbell. In talking with the friends of O'Neil, he learned the woman had confided to them her fear of Ted when she had broken off with him. O'Neil had also believed he had done something to his wife.

Osbourn saw movement at a nearby window and knew he had been observed. Just as he was beginning to wonder if Ted was going to play the "nobody home" game, he heard the lock click and Ted opened the door.

Watching for tell-tale signs of stress, or undue tension, the cop in Osbourn saw the white knuckles, the film of perspiration on the upper lip. Ted was good at controlling himself in spite of feeling nervous, and angry, when he recognized Osbourn on his front step.

"Yes?" was all he said.

"Mind answering a few questions?" was put mildly by Osbourn.

"About what?" was as close to a snap as it could get.

"Mind if I come in while we talk," came out pleasantly.

"Yes, as a matter of fact, I do mind. I'm busy."

"Well, then, since you prefer to talk downtown, that will do as well, since your ribs are better?"

"What are you talking about? What about my ribs?" Ted was unable to keep the surprise from his face or voice.

"It's about your wife, Martha. We'll be expecting you as soon as you can be there."

Needing time to think things through, Ted agreed to appear at the station. Playing the innocent act, he asked "So you've found her?" He needed time to think out every possibility.

The questioning of Ted at the police station covered the past as well as the present. The discovery of Martha Sweltzer living in Decorah for three years as Marti Gracek, her maiden name, re-opened their investigation with the new information.

That she had run again following the bungled "burglary" was reminiscent of the failed abduction three years earlier resulting in her voluntary disappearance at that time. Since then, individuals had come forward, all verifying Ted had been abusive and threatening to his wife in the extreme. Now police wanted to know where he was on the night of the attempted burglary; and how he sustained the injuries to his ribs, knee, and ankle. On being asked to show the mark on his arm where the band aid had been, Ted exploded, furiously charging the police of deliberately accusing him of things he had nothing to do with. Now he demanded a lawyer. With that statement, Ted left the station.

Ted's fury didn't abate by having a lawyer to keep the police at arm's length. It meant more of his money was evaporating because of Martha.

CHRIS LOSINSKI

Osbourn sat at his desk rolling his pen absent-mindedly between his fingers. He stared at the pile of papers he had gone over so many times. Nothing could be solidly pinned on Ted Sweltzer; but so much swirled around the man that it painted him as something awfully bad hiding in plain sight. The officer feared for the safety of Martha, as well as her friend, Shirley. Enough so that he had assigned men to surveil as long as possible, but for any length of time was just not going to happen. It was one thing to suspect things, something else entirely to prove.

Ted kept up a regular routine at his place of business and managed to keep the façade in place of the charming, friendly businessman who loved his work. Ted was well-aware he was being watched by the police. Until he felt safer, he would not make the trip to the storage rental for the photo album—something that he fixated on increasingly. He needed revenge on Martha, the catalyst that was responsible for the downward spiral of his formerly perfect life.

The weeks dragged by as his ribs mended. He limped as he paced during his time off, in the small space available, filled with frustration, impatiently trying to outwait the damn police keeping an eye on him. At least the money was coming in again.

Chris had been spending more nights on the fold-out in his office than in his more comfortable residence. He felt restless and couldn't apply himself to his craft as he had in the past. He struggled to get the old interest back, but too often found himself seated on a wooden stair step periodically whistling for, and calling, Gully. The days were slipping away emptily. Neither Chris nor the Iversons interfered with Gully but watched with sadness as the dog set its own routine, avoiding everyone, staying out of sight, waiting. Chris had propped the pet flap open several nights to help the dog adjust to entering, as evidenced by the empty food bowl he had left where Marti put it. Both he and Thora kept his dish full.

After almost four months had dragged by and Chris finished filling Gully's dish and water bowl for the night, he had checked the rooms over and realized Gully had been sleeping on Marti's bed and pillow.

Another week passed with no news from Shirley or the police on Marti. Chris opened a can of stain and picked up a brush, only to put it all away again, too weighed down with a depression unusual for him. Going out to the wooden steps he had slowly seated himself, and with elbows braced on his knees, rested his head in his hands where he remained unmoving for a long period of time. It had been years since he had felt such utter hopelessness. He struggled to remind himself that he had come through to the other side then, and Godwilling, both he and Marti, wherever she was, would make it out again.

The hardness of the step, as well as weariness, forced him to raise his head, preparing to rise. Sitting on his haunches with his one good front leg braced, was Gully, watching him steadily from perhaps fifteen feet away. And Chris felt the first small glimmer of hope since he had returned from meeting with Marti's family.

As the weeks passed, Chris kept in regular contact with Shirley, Nancy Bolin, and with Officer Tate Osbourn in Des Moines, who confirmed it was not a closed case, and Ted Sweltzer's activities were not going un-noticed by the police. Marti had not made contact with anyone.

Gully began to eat during the day when Chris brought out his own lunch along with a bowl of dog food and they ate together under the overhang in nice weather with Chris careful not to invade the space the dog needed between them. He was grateful for the silent presence of the animal, who at the end of each day slowly climbed the steps to the empty apartment above the shop, and Chris went into the shop for the night and only occasionally to his residence.

In the dark of the night his mind conjured up every possible path, place, person that Marti could have taken, or called on for help. He often considered making a trip to Des Moines, but always the realization it would be pointless, solve nothing and had no leads to anything, kept him from following through on that impulse.

Thora made rare trips up to Henry's old quarters to be sure all was in good order and was well aware Gully was camping there. It was evident he was sleeping on Marti's bed from how dirty the blanket had become. She used a brush to clean off the fur, and shook the blanket, but didn't wash it. She knew the dog found comfort in the familiar scent. Thora had found Marti's record book of clients and given it to Chris. Together they had talked over whether they should say anything to the people she had worked for and decided Marti would want some explanation given. She seemed to have formed friendships with some.

Thora accompanied Chris to the Rasmusson home and saw firsthand the beautiful rosemaled benches on each side of the blue door that Marti was so taken with. Nels had answered the door and, on learning their mission, had invited them in to meet Emma, his wheelchair-bound wife, and to explain to them together why Marti had quit without a word. They had been devastated, and hurt, but as Thora and Chris gently explained why Marti had left as she did, Nels put an arm over his wife's shoulders; then taking a handkerchief from his pocket, gently wiped her tears, and then his own.

At the door, Nels quietly thanked the bearers of sad news, saying it helped to know what happened. They would pray for Marti.

The two had then gone on to the second name on the list, Roxann Truman. When the woman understood what they were there for, she didn't wait for any explanation but told them in no uncertain terms she would see to it Marti never found another job in Decorah. And finished by slamming the door in their faces.

Thora declined to accompany Chris to Sena Dahl's. Chris, if he'd been asked, would have admitted to dreading still another client to face. It took two trips to the Dahl residence to find Sena home, but at least it wasn't like the Truman episode. Sena had invited Chris in when he had said he was there about Marti. She had been genuinely distressed for Marti. Her bubbly, smiley nature had faded until Sena was sitting on her littered couch, silent and downcast, and all the while a cat sat on an end table hissing and spitting, ears back and tail lashing at Chris the whole time. So! This was the "Miss Narci Sistic" Marti had talked about, and they all had laughed over.

At the door as Chris was leaving, Sena asked him to please let her know how Marti was when he learned anything. The bank had been quick and business-like. The manager had thanked Chris for his considerateness. They were deeply sorry to lose her services. She had been an exemplary employee.

Waiting was all Chris--and Gully, could do. He resigned himself to keeping his hands busy with his wood craft but shutting his thoughts off was impossible.

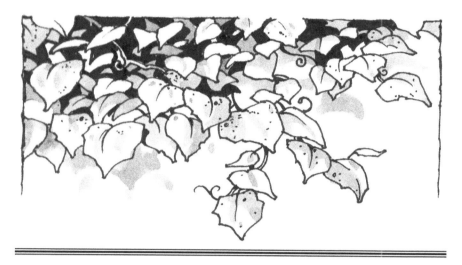

ROAD TO VENGEANCE

Nearly six months had passed since Ted's disastrous trip to Decorah after Archie had tipped him off on Martha. His ribs had healed, and he thought the police had finally given up watching, or following him, but he still wasn't easy about going to the storage rental in search of the album. Archie seemed to have pretty much dropped from sight since he'd broken his ankle. Word had reached Ted it was a bad break and had left the cop with a limp.

But finally, in a most unexpected way, the chance was presented for Ted to get his errand for the album accomplished.

Wencel Sweltzer appeared to be slipping mentally as well as physically. Ted had observed the "old man's" memory wasn't as good as it had been for a while, but his father had still always been in his office, working at his desk without fail until one morning he didn't show up, nor did he answer his home phone.

Ted made a fast trip from the office to his childhood home, letting himself in with the key he had retained. Wencel had fallen in the bathroom, hitting his head on the edge of the tub and rolling onto the floor, where a puddle of blood pooled and coagulated from a cut to his head. He had been unconscious for a short while but was on his feet and cleaning himself up at the sink by the time Ted walked in; but still needed to be seen by a doctor and have several sutures on the side of his head. It was the doctor's orders to rest at home for a day or two and be observed. Leaving Wencel in the housekeeper's care, Ted took the old man's car keys to make sure he didn't leave and was about to leave himself and return to the office when he instead left his own car parked in front of the house, and getting into his father's car, drove off.

And that was the day Ted had driven out to the rental unit, where he spent more time and sweat than he wanted before unearthing the small nightstand. But, at last, the old album was in his hands, and he hoped it held the key to Martha's past that would point him in her direction. The only reason he hadn't destroyed it could be attributed to the chaos and disorder the police (and Audra) had caused to disrupt his life: forcing him to hire movers to take everything to storage while he sold the house.

His small kitchenette was cluttered with unwashed dishes; and a trash bag by the sink was overflowing with the trash from fast food and soft drinks. He had to clear space on the table to be able to go through the album.

The woman who had been cleaning and washing up for Ted had simply quit without a word of warning. He had no clue she resented his demeaning treatment and language to the point that the day came when she simply stopped in her tracks as she faced his door, and after a few moments turned around and walked away.

Ted had been going through each photo looking for anything that might be a clue to something, a place, or town that might have an appeal, or draw, for Martha; going over it again, and again, until he lost patience and began tearing out photos he deemed as useless. On seeing writing on the backs of some, Ted calmed himself, becoming more attentive, and began removing each photo to read what might be on the back. And slowly he began to put together a time--a town that had been a happy place for Martha. Before he met her. On the back of a photo of a placid lake with a wooden swim float not far from a stone-walled point of land with a tall cross at the very end, inscribed with the words, "Inspiration Point." One other photo was of a laughing teenage boy in front of a Ferris wheel. On the back was written, "Del, Red Wing, Minn."

With the cunning instinct of a predator, Ted centered on Minnesota. Red Wing.

He began making plans on how to leave un-noticed, to minimize his absence from work. He had recently promoted a top salesman to a managerial position with a substantial wage increase. He had let it be known he would be spending more time with family as his father needed more attention.

SIX MONTHS EARLIER:
RED WING

When everyone had taken themselves from her rooms and she had heard the police drive off, Marti went into action, pulling the wheeled suitcase from under the bed and filling it with the bare essentials of clothes and personal care items. It was as if she had been rehearsing for this moment for the past three years. She had never put any of her wages in a bank. Now it was in the money belt with the unspent portion of Ted's money. As before, some was kept out and handy.

Reaching under the pillow, Marti wrapped her fingers around a palm-sized jagged rock that she slipped in her jacket pocket, then penned a note to Chris and filled Gully's bowls, leaving them by the table where he was used to finding food and water. As she took a last look around what had been "home" for a while, she heard a faint whimper at the door.

Her relief that he was alright made her cry and she opened the door for him, then held out her hands to him, kneeling. Leaning into her, he licked her wet face and she sat on the floor stroking his head, murmuring to him. Then rising, she held one hand, palm out, to him and said, "stay." The door she propped open. The note to Chris was stuck in his office door; then she wheeled her bike to the sidewalk, knowing Ted was gone, for Gully would not have returned otherwise. Now she rode quickly, guided by streetlight until she reached Phelps park and vanished into the natural undergrowth where she remained (until daylight brought people and traffic around again. Leaving the bicycle in the brush, Marti walked casually out of the park and to the bus station where she bought a ticket south to Peoria, Illinois, but got off at a small bus stop miles before Peoria, buying a new ticket to Davenport, Iowa; again, getting off at another small bus depot half-way to that city. With a third such maneuver, Marti hoped her course was too twisted to follow and wearily boarded a bus for Red Wing, Minnesota.

The small, unobtrusive figure never attracted more than a disinterested glance, if even that. Having been through this routine before had a calming effect on Marti, and she went about finding a simple diner to eat in, which was not hard. Borrowing their phonebook, she searched for a close hotel or motel for the night as she waited for her order. She would need a room for maybe two nights. Exhaustion was making itself felt. She desperately needed sleep.

Checking in at the small hotel desk, she registered for two nights using her maiden name again, "Marti Gracek." She had accepted that Ted would continue looking for her. So be it. One of them would have to die. Her hand rested in her pocket. She wouldn't make it easy for him.

In her room, she braced a chairback under the doorknob, then showered, rinsed out the clothing she wore and hung them up to dry overnight. Then she climbed into bed and slept for hours.

The search for work began the first day as Marti made her way back to the small restaurant. As she walked, she observed life moving on around her from behind the dark glasses. She watched as a man rose from the bench on the corner to move towards an approaching city bus, tossing a newspaper into a wire receptacle which Marti whisked out as she passed, barely pausing.

Inside the restaurant, in the most private booth she could find, Marti studied the "Work Wanted" and job openings section as she waited for her breakfast. She still carried Shirley's letter of recommendation: she knew she couldn't use any of her former clients for referrals. She considered looking for something besides housecleaning, but what would that be? She also needed to find a less expensive place to stay than a hotel or motel but read of nothing in the paper.

As she left the small restaurant, she made a mental note to herself to keep her eyes open for a different place to eat. This one hadn't been particularly good. Looking around, the town seemed so different to her now. Everything changes of course, twenty years makes a difference—no surprise there! Some things seemed familiar though: the way the streets would sometimes rise, or dip. It was an old city, lots of brick; interesting.

But she hadn't seen all that much of it back then, either. There had been a fair going on that one summer, out on the edge of town, set up on a level area. And she had seen that only at night all lit up. So many years ago. Did they still have fairs?

As she walked, she read signs in windows in a few places;

some wanting waiters, or dishwashers. One was for a cook. Hmm. She remembered shopping for her school clothes in one or two dress shops on the one day she and the other young workers were brought in a van by "Pops" who, with his wife, managed the Frontenac Bible Camp on Lake Pepin. It had been a happy, magical time in her life the two summers she had been accepted to work there. At breakfast every morning, the older couple had read aloud to the long table lined with young workers. "Moms" had read from a booklet called, "The Upper Room." Now she thought about the words, "In quietness and trust is your strength" and "I have not forgotten you."

She walked on, acquainting herself with the historic city and, by noon, found herself tired and hungry in a small city park, filled with lush growth, winding paths, benches, a drinking fountain, and an ornate, unique looking food stand not far from a corner. An old man dozed in the sun on a bench along the sidewalk, not far from the stand. Bird chatter could be heard in trees. Marti passed on soft rubber soles, seemingly un-noticed and paused at the beautifully painted food stand where an older man in a white apron tied around a generous middle turned a friendly smile in her direction, his blue eyes not missing much, and asked her what she'd like. As she read the menu listing several sandwiches, hotdogs, chips, candy bars, and more, she heard the owner's voice; still pleasant but lowered, speak to someone else. "Not now, Rolo." Turning, Marti saw the old man, who had seemed asleep in the sun, had approached her but at the words of, "Not now, Rolo" had turned away and was ambling back to the bench. Rolo was a bum.

"Yes'm, you were sayin'?" drew her attention back to all that was displayed in the clean and tidy stand.

"Two hotdogs, please. With everything. And a bag of popcorn." Marti knew she didn't fool the man behind the counter. As she paid for her food, he had turned his friendly gaze on her and given a respectful nod.

Turning around and looking for another bench, she passed close enough to Rolo to stretch out a hand with the wrapped hotdog, offering it to him. He lifted his shaggy head far enough to make eye contact and held up a hand with stained fingernails for the food, and she heard a mumbled, "T'anks," and noted missing teeth at the same time.

Finding a bench further into the park, Marti sat down to eat and rest. It was welcoming there; trees and bushes formed a green backdrop behind the bench, with sidewalk path in front.

To the left, across the street were old but well-kept homes. The neat lawns were raised several feet higher than the sidewalk, held back by an old stone retaining wall. As she finished her hotdog, Marti studied the large old homes, noting that the house on the right, on the corner, had stairs attached to the side that led to an entrance on the second level. This had to be rentals. Individual rooms? Small apartments? Her eyes drifted upward to the ornate windows and odd-shaped round rooms that rose from ground level to a third floor with a conical roof. A fascinating building. She wanted a closer look before leaving the park.

Opening the popcorn, Marti tossed a few kernels towards the sidewalk for birds. Feeding the active, energetic tiny creatures always brought a calmness to her; and it never seemed to take her long to lure them to the popcorn. Rested and relaxed, Marti scattered the remaining popcorn and rose from the bench, causing a flurry of wings. Bending over the drinking fountain, Marti was grateful for the clear, cold water. Wanting to know more about the historic looking house on the corner, she crossed the street to the steps that passed through the retaining wall to a terrace style walk leading upwards to an ornate Victorian door with a heavy iron knocker that sounded with a "boom" in Marti's ear when she lifted and released it, giving her a childish urge to run. No sound came from the other side of the door, and as she thought about using the knocker again, or retreating, a disembodied voice reached her ears.

"You will need to do that two more times, with force. Fay is extremely hard of hearing."

With her eyes raking back and forth in the general direction of the voice, Marti found herself stuttering, at a loss for words.

"Oh! Well, uh, yes--uh, thanks—I, uh—thanks." She had finally seen the pale face of an elderly woman beneath the leaves of a tree, framed by low branches. Giving a gentle nod and a soft, "You're welcome," the pale face was gone.

Squaring her shoulders and taking a deep breath, Marti grabbed the knocker and banged it twice without holding back, her face reddening with embarrassment. But the advice she had been given was right on the mark. Someone was thumping their way to the door, which, when it had opened on squealing hinges, revealed a wrinkled face framed in tightly permed blue hair. One arthritic hand held the door open—and the other gripped a very ornate, gold-headed man's walking stick.

"There's no need to beat the door down, Miss!" was spoken in what could only be called a shout.

What followed for Marti was the most difficult conversation she had ever encountered, but she persisted, resorting to shouting with great enunciation; and finally, a chalk board was produced after she was invited to follow Mrs. Hessel leading the way into a Victorian furnished room giving a view of the street and park from the round end of the room.

Fay Hessel did indeed have two rental apartments on the second level, both rented, the one resident was recovering from a broken leg in a nursing home several blocks away, until he could manage on his own again. As the chatty landlady revealed how the poor man not only had his vintage car totaled in the unfortunate incident, but his driving license had been revoked, Marti recognized Mrs. Hessel was making the most of her unexpected company.

Marti's disappointment at word of no vacancy was evident but she thanked the congenial woman and rose from the Victorian loveseat she had been seated on, preparing to leave. But Fay remained in her overstuffed chair, a thoughtful expression on the wrinkled face.

"You don't party, do you? And no men, understand?" she roared. The lady could sound rough and tough, but she had a kind heart; and the thin pixie-faced woman sitting on Fay's loveseat touched her heart. Marti sank back on the brocade seat and speechlessly shook her head at the questions.

Lifting one arthritis-deformed hand towards Marti, Mrs. Hessel began explaining the condition of the small rooms on the third floor at a volume that likely could be heard through the front door.

It had been servants' quarters at one time. Mrs. Hessel couldn't climb the stairs anymore, but the last time she had seen it, there was only a wooden rope bed, and a low dresser up there. It had needed cleaning then and was no doubt worse now. There was a light fixture with a plugin, but the bathroom consisted of a chain pull commode, a small sink and a mini tub, that a plumber would have to tend to first. The rent would need to cover electricity, heat, and water. Something could be worked out.

Rapidly tabulating the potential difference between the offer, the hotel, or to keep looking for a single room, Marti chose the servants' quarters. The renters on the second floor shared a communal bathroom Marti could use until the plumber had the third-floor plumbing in working order. Mrs. Hessel's grandson, Gordon, came by to check on her every day after school, and on weekends. He was expected any minute and would show her around if she was interested.

Marti had slept on the floor of a church bell tower. She had slept in a park, sheltering under bushes and trees. She had slept on buses. This sounded better than anything she had already gone through.

Fay's grandson had shown up as expected, a high school senior as outgoing as his grandmother. He had come in through a back door to the kitchen after leaving his bike leaning against the porch rail.

He had led Marti up the outside steps to an open-sided porch with rockers and a table, arranged and waiting for the residents. After explaining the outside door was to be locked by sundown, they had entered a long hallway where Gordon pointed out three doors; the first was the renters' communal bathroom, the other two were apartments belonging to two elderly men, one a bachelor, the other a widower. Directing her to the left where the light was dim, hidden from sight were narrow steps that rose steeply to a tiny landing before a door with old iron hinges and door latch. Gordon produced an antiquated key to unlock it, and loud creaks could be heard as he pushed the door open.

"I'll oil those hinges before I leave," he promised, grinning as he gave the door a couple more opening and closings.

The odd shapes of the room in the servant's quarters came from the angles of the roof, with most of the light coming from the odd round area at the front of the house, with some light coming from smaller round windows in several alcoves.

Marti wandered, big-eyed, through the echoing, bare rooms. The sloping ceilings were head bumpers, but otherwise the central areas gave plenty of head room.

The round room had adequate height and gave a wonderful view of street and park. It all smelled of dust and age, buried in quietness. Marti left feeling jubilant.

Not much of the day was left as Marti walked back the way she had come, keeping an eye out for some homey-looking eating place. Not much had caught her attention until she spotted a small, white, house-like building with a packed parking area. On closer examination of the place, it appeared to have been a gas station at one time, and an addition had been added to it.

Inside the small eatery, Marti looked quickly around and knew she had no pick of spot this time. She made a beeline for the first vacancy she saw: a stool at the red-topped bar, and in seconds was perched on a stool with a matching red plastic top, knowing what her order would be. There was a short wait before her grilled cheese and milk arrived in spite of the fast and efficient servers.

Marti couldn't shake the unease that filled her in the new surroundings as she walked the distance to her hotel. Fewer cars passed in the street, and most pedestrians were gone to their homes. It was a lonely time of the day. Light was dimming, and Marti's hands were in her jacket pockets, the right hand wrapped around the "rock." She made herself as un-noticeable as she could while wishing she were back at the hotel. She needed to buy another bike—it made getting around so much easier, and right now she could feel the tiredness throughout her entire body.

There would be a number of things needing to be dealt with the next day. Most important would be the hunt for work, but the bike was needed to speed things along.

After bracing a chairback under the doorknob, Marti made use of the phone book provided in the room and using the small notepad and pencil from the drawer of the bedside stand, she wrote addresses next to items she needed to look for. Beginning with a used bike. With baskets.

Marti walked herself back to Ed's Eatery for breakfast, deciding they were worth the effort; and was early enough to get a booth for two that had been squeezed into a nook beyond the counter, and soon she was enjoying a bowl of oatmeal, a banana and coffee.

The door had jingled frequently as customers came and left; almost everyone was greeted by Ed behind the counter and cash register, causing Marti to glance up from beneath her hat brim frequently. As she was finishing, the door jingled again and Ed called out a warm "Hey, Kathy! How ya doin'?" and Marti glancing up again, froze at the sight of a female police officer. "Heard you were in a scuffle the other evening. You okay?" Ed had continued his questions without waiting for an answer. Now he pointed a finger in the direction of the policewoman's forehead and remarked, "I see you still have a little bump there, turning green."

"I'm, fine, Ed, thanks. Got that in a little "dust-up." Just sorry the kid turned a simple shoplift into assault. He felt bad about it later."

"I'll bet he did. Comes from real fine people. Devastated." With more bell sounds, Ed excused himself while Kathy sat at the counter and the waitress called to her in passing, "Same thing, Kathy?" who responded with "You bet."

Waiting until the officer's breakfast had her occupied, Marti slipped to the cash register, silently paid her bill to the affable Ed, and left.

Kathy's head had turned at the sound of the doorbell and her dark eyes had followed the small figure through the window hurrying away, head lowered, face shadowed.

Marti feared the police, feared being recognized, of having Ted's attention drawn to her. There was no way for her to completely change her identity, or to simply melt away into the crowds, or a busy city. To live, she needed others. For work, food, shelter. As she hurried away from a place she would have liked to frequent for good meals, she felt weighted with discouragement, knowing she would not return there.

"Think about the bike," she scolded herself. "That's next! Do it! And look for a church with a clothes closet—you need clothes. Get busy! Get busy!"

Following the address and notes she had written to herself, Marti found the sports store, and they did have secondhand, refurbished, not so stylish bikes in a shop attached to the back of the two-story, narrow brick building. It reeked of age. Feeling under pressure and very unsettled, she examined the few choices available and made a quick decision, asking to have large bike baskets attached before she left. She paced the aisles as she waited, unusual for her; it would take at least a half-hour. Near the front of the store, she turned around to avoid two loiterers catching up with each other's lives, and she overheard the scattered words of "—so need help!" and "—hiring nurse aids" and then, "—it's a good nursing home."

The words "hiring, nurse aids" had stopped her in her tracks. That was work that had not occurred to her. Hadn't Mrs. Hessel mentioned a nursing home a few blocks from what was about to become "home" for her? Looking for clothes could wait.

The bike would quickly get her to the nursing home in time to fill out an application yet today! Red Wing was big enough to have more than one nursing home, but that would be easy to find out when she asked for an application form. Suddenly, the day seemed to vastly improve, a weight lifted, and Marti felt hopeful again.

The bike had cost a little more than she had liked, but once she was pedaling her way through town in the direction of the park she was pleased with the bike's performance. At the sports store, Marti had purchased a blow-up air mattress, as well as a cheap sleeping bag with a small pillow, planning to be at the Hessel residence by the time Gordon was there. Surely, he would have a bicycle tire pump to inflate the blow-up mattress. She had opted not to spend money on one. If she missed him, she could count on a very uncomfortable night. As she pedaled between the park and her new residence, she was unaware of being watched curiously by not one, but two individuals.

The nursing home was set back from the street on a well-tended expanse of green grass and several flourishing young trees. There was a bike rack considerately set under the covered walk-entrance, and she secured her bike there with several others. She had taken the precaution of leaving nothing in the baskets when she had reached "home."

The building seemed quite new; a brick, one-story, three-winged building with a welcoming lobby. A glass-enclosed directory informed her of the office location. It was with trepidation Marti turned the doorknob and entered a quiet, neat and organized office area with a secretary seated behind a closed sliding glass window that opened as she approached. The neatly dressed young woman behind the desk openly assessed the slight, shy figure in front of her, asking how she could be of help. Suddenly all Marti's confidence deserted her, and she almost turned to leave. It was not easy for her asking to fill out an application form for a job she had no experience in, but somehow, she did.

There! It was out! She had no experience. To her surprise, the young woman had smiled, pushed the form out to Marti and said, "We provide the training if you fill this out and are accepted."

Her knees felt wobbly as she made her way to a chair with the clipboard and pen fastened by a chain to the board. For thirty minutes she wrote and thought. And thought and wrote, sticking as much to the truth as she could without giving herself away. Marti believed that staying with truth in all ways possible while staying safe was the best course she could follow. Turning the clipboard and form in at the window, the girl pointed out the lack of a phone number, but when Marti explained she had just arrived in town and was moving into the new address on the form this very night, she would have no phone until she could afford one. The girl had begun to look doubtfully at Marti but asked if she could come for an interview the next Monday afternoon at two-thirty.

Marti was free to settle in over the weekend and she could only hope to have a job after Monday. Thanking the girl for helping her, she left hoping the food stand was operating. Her stomach was growling, and she needed a little quiet time to think everything over and plan for the next errand.

Spending time in a park was renewing for Marti and she was grateful for the lovely little "natureland" so close to where she would live and work. She loved the feel of a fresh breeze in her face, and the warmth of the sun through the jacket on her shoulders was almost like a friend's arm. She found a bench more secluded further into the small park where sun shining through the branches had warmed a spot for Marti to sit and eat her sandwich with chips and a cold lemonade. She took her time, letting the peace-and-quiet clear her mind and lift her spirits.

Relaxed and refreshed she gathered the wrappings from her meal, tossing them into a trash receptacle, and tucked the banana into a pocket. Taking the time to appreciate nature, and the birds, it was a leisurely walk leaving the park.

To all appearances Rolo seemed asleep, stretched out on the bench near the food stand where Marti had seen him the day before. An open newspaper concealed his face from curious eyes, but Rolo was aware of everything going on near him, he'd glimpsed Marti's soundless approach, had noted the near-stop at the foot of the bench and then her passing on. When she exited the park and crossed the street to the Hessel house, Rolo folded his paper and sitting up reached for the banana lying near his feet.

And neither Rolo, nor Marti were aware of someone quietly watching, wondering.

MINCEMEAT

Gordon wouldn't be checking on his grandmother for at least an hour which left Marti wondering about the wisdom of trying to take care of any other errands. She needed to talk with the young man—it was too difficult making Fay understand Marti's questions. The grandson could expedite things like borrowing a broom, bucket, mop, rags. And until the plumber fixed the small bathroom, water would need to be carried from the second-floor bathroom. There was a lot of scrubbing needed on the third floor.

Restless with waiting, Marti wandered around the yard

and saw a clothesline in the back yard. Wandering back, she climbed the steps with a thought to parking herself on one of the chairs on the landing and hoped the owners of the chairs wouldn't mind. Halting on the last step, she stared at one of the ugliest cats she had ever seen. It was resting comfortably on one of the cushioned chairs, its paws curled under its chest, its huge body covering most of the chair, a crooked tail hanging over the edge. It didn't move, but turned its one eye on Marti, and perked its one-and-a-half ears in her direction. It was the most beat-up cat Marti had ever seen; obviously a fighter, and she decided to allow it all the space it might want. Backing down a few steps, she turned, and decided to sit on the bottom step to wait for Gordon. She hoped the cat wouldn't turn out to be an impediment when she wanted to access her rooms.

Gordon was there at his usual time, and Marti presented her requests to be given to Mrs. Hessel by the good-natured grandson; then resumed her seat on the bottom step where she waited for answers to her requests. Hardly had she seated herself when she heard the soft thumps of cat paws carrying the overweight feline down the steps towards her, bringing her to her feet. Stepping aside and keeping well away from the battered beast, she watched in fascination as it made its way into the neighboring yard, finding its way through the hedge. Marti shook her head, surprised to feel respectful and admiring of the cat. Curious to know where it had gone, she followed where the animal had disappeared, and found herself looking over the hedge into the yard of the woman who had spoken to her through the tree growth. There were lush bushes around the neighboring house, but no sign of the cat. Behind her she heard the kitchen door open, and the sound of Gordon's feet on the porch. He grinned at Marti and dangled a ring of keys in her direction and told her to follow him as he turned towards the backyard, heading in the direction of a storage shed.

"Gran said to tell you, make use of anything that strikes

your fancy out here." Gordon talked while walking, and un-locking the padlock hanging on the shed's door. The shed was well-stuffed with household furnishings either outdated or broken, jostling for space with regularly used yard tools.

"Take your time in here, Ms. Grace. Gran wants me to pick up a couple things from the grocery store. I can help carry anything you want up the stairs when I get back." Gordon was already heading out the door as Marti asked about the bike tire pump. Was there one in the shed?

"If you don't see one goin' over things, I have one at home that I can bring tomorrow." And then he was gone.

She could only hope one crossed her path as she looked through the discarded furnishings, accumulated over the years. There were worse things than sleeping on a floor. The one thing she wanted more than the tire pump was a chair. Even a broken chair. Just one that could be lodged beneath a doorknob. Without that, Marti knew sleep would escape her.

Now she stood and looked searchingly into nooks and crannies belonging to spiders. Moving slowly around the clut-ter, she found a bucket, and after examining it for holes, set it outside the shed door. The small kitchen table was hard to identify under the mess as it lay upside down with one of its legs lying on its underside. It took a while freeing it, to lay it out on the ground by the bucket. One of the boxes that had rested on it had rattled ominously and she had opened it to see broken crockery. She had taken the time to pick through it and found a few whole dishes, plates, cup and one bowl, that she set aside. An old—very old—cupboard was stuffed with junk, half-buried in debris which Marti painstakingly cleared and tried to pull towards the door but, lacking the strength, had to leave the job to Gordon. It wasn't a large cupboard, but narrow, rustic. She was keeping in mind the narrow, steep stairs and odd-shaped "attic." A small, battered table was found for beside the bed, and then two chairs came into view, both missing their cane seats. No problem there—one for the door; and placing a board over the seat of the other Marti had a chair for at the table. Perfect.

She was so engrossed she hadn't heard Gordon when he had walked in holding a tire pump and wearing a big grin. "I was close to home, so I picked it up." Marti almost hugged him.

"I'm so sorry to have disturbed everything so much. I'll try to get it all back into place. I think this might be enough. For now, anyway—still need broom and mop," Marti smiled back at Gordon.

Between the two of them, they carried the old furniture up narrow stairs to the third floor. Nothing seemed to faze the young man, who called her Ms. Grace, which she chose not to correct. He was quick in inflating her air mattress and she gratefully thanked him. As he finished hauling up what was usable to Marti, she recalled the scary-looking cat that had unnerved her earlier on the porch deck, and she questioned him on how she should respond to the animal should it return.

Gordon laughed gregariously and enjoyed enlightening her. "Aw, that's Mincemeat! He's harmless. Stupid, actually. Doesn't know he shouldn't fight with dogs. Lost an eye that way. Ear, too, I guess."

"He's safe to pet, then?" Marti asked.

"Oh, sure. But he'll be a pest if you do. Well, I gotta let Gran know what's goin' on. Here's your door key, Ms. And this one is for the outside door that has to be locked by sundown." With mission accomplished, Fay's grandson bounded down the wooden stairs.

Marti walked slowly towards the tower room, dragging a chair towards the curved window over-looking the park. Placing an old metal cookie sheet across the cane-less chair seat, she sat down, gazing out at the lovely little park in the slowly changing light, her thoughts finally turning to all she had left behind. Chris. Gully. The Iversons. And all the people she had worked for--even Roxann Truman. Some she cared so much for it hurt. The tears had come then, along with stifled sobs.

Old bed slats had been found in the shed and these Marti placed across the bed covering them with a discarded canvas, and then placed the inflated air mattress on top. Opening the sleeping bag, she spread that on her "bed."

Then she left, locking her door behind her, the dark glasses hiding her eyes—puffy and pink from weeping. She needed to make a quick trip to the nearest grocery store where she bought packaged food that would keep for her supper and breakfast. Marti had found old tins in the shed to store food in; if there were mice, she did not want to attract them. Marti had temporary use of the bathroom on the second floor until the plumber finished work in her own small bathroom, come Monday. Her interview at the nursing home was Monday afternoon, which meant she had to leave her rooms unlocked if the plumber was still there when she leaves.

As Gordon raced off on his bike, his mind was on the schoolwork waiting at home, as well as the new girl in his English class, a pretty redhead. Traffic was a little heavier as the good citizens of Red Wing headed for home and their dinners at the end of the day. The tap-tap of a horn near him brought his attention back to the moment and he looked towards the sound, ready to apologize, and recognized Officer Kathy.

"Pay attention, Gord," came out the rolled down window from a smiling face framed in dark curls. She had pulled to the curb, so Gordon turned his bike around and came close to the car window of the officer. "How's your grandmother doing? Heard she has a new renter."

"She's doin' fine—deaf as a doorknob though! You know!"

"Heard she's renting out the third floor. How's that going?"

"Kind of fun, really. Moved the lady in today. She travels light."

"What's her name, if you don't mind my asking?"

Gordon frowned, concentrating and gave a small shake of the head, then doubtfully said, "Grace. Yeah, Grace. Uhhh-Mary! Yeah, that's it! Mary Grace." Gordon had finally remembered the new renter's name. Incorrectly. Grinning, he told the officer to "take care" and pedaled on home, his mind back on the redhead.

Marti had opened her door early in the morning, leaving it open, and had listened closely for the resident below to finish his ablutions so she could get in a fast shower, and wash out the few clothes she had. She had no choice but to find the church closets available in the area and do her "shopping" there this morning.

The two-thirty p.m. interview occupied her mind. If she was not accepted, she needed to find any other nursing homes where she would have to go through the whole process all over again. The find-a-job urgency was beginning to feel all-consuming.

Marti had slept well in the unfamiliar surroundings, with the streetlight providing a surprising amount of visibility for her.

Hearing her neighbor vacate the bathroom at the base of her stairs, she had quickly gone down to shower, and prepare for the day. Her breakfast had been a small jar of mixed fruit, and a sweet roll. A cup of coffee would have been so nice. Water from a fruit jar was all that was to be had "for the present," but garage and yard sales could produce some nice surprises. Maybe a coffee pot would eventually turn up. There was a lot of cleaning to be done but had to wait for now.

By nine a.m. Marti was on her bike and looking for the address of a church where a clothes closet might be. She had been raised Lutheran, though she knew her Dad had grown up Methodist: she knew the Methodist—as well as others—had clothing for those who needed help. She had grown up expecting to help others in need and ended up being one of the needy. It hurt, but one could only play the hand they are dealt. "Keep your head up, Marti," she kept reminding herself.

Marti's morning "shopping" had been rewarding which had the effect of lightening her mood. As she neared home, she looked towards the food stand, and thought about the coffee she had longed for earlier. It was almost lunch time anyway. A sandwich and fruit would be nice with coffee. She had dismounted from the bike, taking her time pushing it along the walk while looking around for Rolo.

Standing in front of the friendly food stand owner, Marti ordered a ham sandwich, an apple, and a large coffee. Waiting, she quietly commented on Rolo's absence.

"Haven't seen him today, but he kind of comes and goes, like the wind. He was here last night."

Marti made a little nod acknowledging the forthcoming information. As she paid for her order, and reached for it, the friendly owner spoke again. "I'm Martin, by the way. Heard Fay had a real nice new renter."

She hoped Martin hadn't noticed her hesitation before answering, "I'm Marti. Nice to meet you. It's a marvelous park you have here. Very peaceful." To herself she added, "Stop talking. That's enough." Then picking up her order and nodding to the man, Marti wheeled her bike to the bench across from her new apartment and settled herself for a quiet lunch.

Unaware of someone silently watching, wondering.

The interview was over, and Marti would be reporting for training immediately, even while being oriented to the job learning bed baths; helping to feed those needing assistance. Blue uniforms were required, and she had been directed to first look at the used uniforms in a second-hand store where she found a small size uniform in good condition. She needed to have an extra one, but might have to order that, something she had hoped to avoid. While trying on the uniform in the small cubicle, she had seen that she again needed a haircut, which she couldn't keep putting off. It was a job she particularly disliked. She had bought the hair shears at a yard sale shortly after arriving in Decorah and had by trial-and-error slowly learned to give herself a passable haircut. One more thing on her to-do list for the day.

A chatty clerk in the "Handy Hand-Me-Down's" had recommended what she considered to be a good place to eat when Marti had asked for a good reference. The girl had told Marti her favorite place to eat was the "Kitchen Sink." Their burgers were the absolute best, according to her. And so was the chicken potpie. And peach cobblers. And the ...." It appeared the clerk had tried everything and liked it all. Marti decided to try "The Kitchen Sink" that evening and was glad to know it wasn't that far away. Leaving the second-hand shop, she made a quick stop at a hardware store she had seen nearby for glue and twine needed to put the leg back on the table.

Back in her room, Marti gave herself the despised haircut and was glad when it was over, and she hadn't done too bad a job of it. It was an easier job gluing the leg back into the tabletop and setting it upright with twine wrapping the leg tightly to the table body, leaving it to dry beneath the hanging light bulb. Maybe a yard sale would eventually turn up a toaster and a coffee maker.

The plumber had worked miracles with the old plumbing, and Marti breathed a sigh of relief. He had commented to her how things used to be made to last.

It had been a full and eventful week for Marti with intensive training in patient care in the nursing home. The work was hard. Turning, lifting, supporting weak and helpless patients was difficult for big, strong aids. For Marti it was more difficult, and she worked to master all the techniques available not only to keep her patients safe, but herself as well.

Following her orientation, she would be on the first shift, which she had hoped for. She was an early riser, ready for work. Her relief was great knowing she would be able to support herself. She had been exhausted at the end of those first weeks of orientation but had finished the trial period with a glowing report.

Day followed day, and quiet, non-intrusive Marti became an accepted sight to the residents of her area. She was often in the park, seen feeding the birds and squirrels. And Rolo. He seemed to have an extra sense when she would come around; and he always left her favorite bench free for her. Mincemeat at times appeared with her, counting on the generosity of his human friend to share her sandwiches with him. He never failed to respond with loud purrs and a busy display of washing his face after feasting. Marti had become acquainted with her downstairs neighbor, William, at the nursing home where he was recovering and getting therapy for his broken leg. When William realized Marti lived upstairs from him, he had upped his talking points for being released home. The stairs were what couldn't be managed, and his friends, as well as a nephew were increasingly promoting the thought of finding a ground floor dwelling.

LUCY RADSTONE

Glad for the fresh air and warm sun. Marti's eyes took in the June flowers in pots and beds all along her route home. Passing the stone retaining wall along the walk, in front of Lucy Radstone's large Victorian home, Marti scanned the yard from behind her dark glasses for the frail woman. Her neighbor recently had been seated in an outdoor rocker, warming herself in the sun, with Mincemeat at her feet, and called out a pleasant "Hello" as Marti passed. And Marti had stopped, looking down at the disfigured cat.

"So! Mincemeat belongs to you?" she had asked, making conversation, and the elderly woman had laughed.

"No. He belongs to himself. I'm just his admirer. And I try to make his life a little easier, which he accepts if it pleases him. I'm Lucy Radstone, by the way."

Something about the thin woman touched Marti causing her to linger, and visit. "Pleased to meet you," she had murmured. "I'm Marti Gracek. I'm sure you know I'm Fay's renter up on the third floor."

"Yes. I had heard. I hope you are liking it there. Fay is a good soul. Talking with everyone always was a great joy for her. Sad for her to lose her hearing."

An inherent kindness seemed to radiate from the pale faced woman. Marti felt as though she was silently being invited to stay. To visit. Looking at her she thought Lucy must have been beautiful in her youth. Her naturally waving silver hair was cut short, the soft curls framing a fine-boned face. She must have been fairly tall at one time, judging from the long-boned limbs, and fingers, the thin wrists and ankles. "Gordon says Mincemeat didn't know enough to leave dogs alone. Looks like he should have learned something." Marti felt safe keeping the cat as center of attention, and Lucy had again given her light laugh.

"He can't be blamed for everything, Marti. His tail for instance. He was hunting birds in the park. Cats do that, you know. But it was a human who didn't keep his dog on a leash. Poor Mince. He could have gone up a tree, I suppose. Maybe he panicked; anyway, he made a run for home, across the street, and that dog caught him by his tail—just before a car ran over the dog."

They had smiled at the irony in the story, but Marti felt compelled to say, "A sad ending for the dog—caused by a human," and Lucy had answered, "It usually is."

Marti had begun looking for Lucy whenever she rode past on her way home from the nursing home.

Marti used her days off cleaning her living space, and hand-washing her few clothes, making use of the old clothesline in the backyard when the weather was nice. She had strung a plastic line in one of the alcoves for rainy days, and of course in winter, should she still be here. She learned to take life one day at a time while keeping alert and being careful.

Hanging out her small laundry on her weekend off, Lucy's voice had barely carried over from the neighboring yard, and Marti could hardly see her peering over the hedge. "Marti, sometimes eating alone is depressing, and I see you occasionally at Martin's stand. If you have no plans for tonight, would you care to join me for dinner? Say, at six o'clock?"

"How nice of you to ask! That sounds more wonderful than you know, Lucy. I would love to." Surprise and happiness resounded in Marti's answer.

Her plans for the afternoon were to get around through the neighborhoods looking for garage and yard sales. She had fixed the old, beat-up table, and scrubbed it well. But on finding left-over paint in the shed, it was now an attractive cream color with a fine black piping around the edges and areas of the legs.

How interesting to Marti were the glimpses into the lives of others the yard sales provided. Each place she stopped, spread out on improvised tables were the no-longer wanted items of daily living; discarded by the inhabitants of that home. She saw their tastes in books, music, games, favorite colors. Sometimes it was simply wanting the newest, or latest style of perfectly good things. Kitchen utensils seemed to be at the top of women's lists. Something Marti had overheard said by a woman at one of the functions Ted had insisted on going to, came up in her memory as she held a "like new" electric coffee pot. "Some women can throw things out the back door faster than a man can bring them in the front door." For $1.50 Marti had her coffee pot. She bought coffee on her way home. The attractive woven placemats for 10 cents protected the newly painted tabletop perfectly. It had been a pleasant, and profitable afternoon, and now she looked forward to a pleasant evening.

Dresses—Marti had none of. She had to be utilitarian, but

she had acquired a dressy pair of slacks and a pretty blouse to wear to Lucy's that evening. The invitation had filled Marti with pleasant anticipation. A meal, a *real* meal. One she hadn't been forced to make and suffer through.

Marti's face showed surprise when Lucy's door opened before she could press the doorbell and a woman she hadn't seen before invited her in.

"Lucy forget to tell you about me? Well, I'm Fern, and I'll be fixing you and Lucy an honest-to-goodness banquet—you can count on it. Go into the living room on your right, can't miss it," and she laughed. Then the plump, beaming Fern bustled towards the back of the house. The hall was broad with gleaming wood floors. An oak hall tree with mirror stood by the front door with umbrellas in a brass cylinder in its center and a matching base on each side for overshoes and hooks above for coats and hats. A cushioned oak bench was along the opposite side by a closed pocket door and a wide stairway rose along that wall with a railing that curved along an upstairs hall. A beautiful chandelier hung from the high ceiling.

A double wide doorway with pocket doors slid back guided Marti into an elegant, inviting living room where her eyes went to her hostess seated in a comfortable chair near a matching sofa, with a glass-topped coffee table in front of it. Heavy drapes had been pulled across the expanse of windows that gave the view of the park. Two beautiful chairs with a small table between them were arranged before the covered windows, with large, thriving plants attractively arranged close to the windows. A fireplace with more seating was at the opposite end of the room.

"I do apologize, Marti, for not welcoming you in. You would think I'd know by now my back does not like me digging in the flower beds," Lucy chuckled softly. "But do come sit down by me and tell how your day has gone! And, by the way, Fern often fixes my meals for me. She's not here every day, but she puts the most wonderful dishes in the freezer, so—actually, I never cook but I am well-fed."

With that the two women found things to talk of: some mundane, some of local events, and activities. And history of the area. Before Marti was even aware, she was revealing a past connection when she'd asked if the fair still came to Red Wing. As soon as Marti had spoken, a stillness came over her and thoughts tumbled around in her head in confusion. Raising her eyes, she saw in Lucy's face nothing but compassion, and a deep sadness in Lucy's eyes. When she spoke, it was softly.

"Marti, I believe you are me forty-eight years ago, and I believe I know what you are going through."

Lucy knew Marti needed space and time, so now she lightened the mood, asking if the younger woman had any interest in cards, and Marti had grimaced.

"Oh! That bad then! Well, that's all right," and Lucy prepared to move on, but Marti had second-thoughts and asked just what games Lucy was interested in.

Lucy listed several.

Marti jumped at one saying, "My parents played Canasta—I'd like to learn that one!"

With the sound of sliding pocket doors across the hall, Fern announced that dinner was served. Lucy struggled to get out of her chair, and when Marti approached her in concern, she did ask for a little assist up. Once on her feet, Lucy's thin hand clung to Marti's arm, but her smile remained as the gracious hostess asked her guest if she'd mind her leaning on Marti on the way to the table.

She moved slowly, and Marti's sympathy was evident. Fern watched, troubled, then put on a scowl as she scolded Lucy for pulling weeds which she should have known better than to do.

To sit at the beautifully laid table, breathing in the aroma of the tastefully presented fare--that she, Marti, had not prepared and served under duress--was a new experience. Sitting across from Lucy, she took it in, wondering how such a wonderful evening could seemingly come out of nowhere. She felt safe here, even after Lucy discerned things that Marti believed she had perfectly concealed.

The conversation flowed easily as they waited for their coffee and dessert. Marti's attention had been drawn to a large portrait of a younger Lucy leaning into a tall, dignified man whose gaze was on her.

"My husband, Phillip. He was a judge, a widower when I met him. I miss him dreadfully. He was a most amazing man, so kind and good." Lucy turned her attention from the portrait to Marti.

"One of the rare ones, my dear, but they do exist," and her pleasant chuckle followed.

The evening had passed so quickly, but Marti had taken the opportunity, as Fern had poured the coffee, to thank the woman for the wonderful dinner.

As Marti offered to assist Lucy on leaving the table, she was aware of the tiredness on the face of the frail woman, and suggested Lucy should be resting her back. When she felt better, they could talk about a game of cards.

With Fern hovering in the background, Lucy smiled, and agreed.

The card games became a weekly occurrence for Marti and Lucy. As summer progressed, so did the friendship between the two women. Marti came to rely on the wisdom of the older woman, and the time came when she confided in Lucy as she had in Shirley. That Lucy opened her own past to her meant so much to Marti. It helped her get past feeling alone with her fear and shame; knowing Lucy had walked in her shoes. And, to see how Lucy's life had turned right side up once she escaped the abusive man she had married.

Lucy encouraged Marti to keep her guard up as there were a type of abusers who would be relentless in their pursuit of any woman who tried to leave.

PROVERBS 20:12

"The hearing ear and the seeing eye--
the Lord has made them both."

Officer Webb pretty much knew most residents of Red Wing. She had a tendency towards perfectionism, and in the process of doing her police work to the best of her ability, she had come to know the people she served very well. She took note of new faces and license plates with interest, which left Marti as a mystery in Kathy's enquiring mind. Kathy noted Marti's use of the park, knew where she boarded, that no one really knew her, but no one could put her down either. She knew where Marti worked. And that her name was Marti Gracek, not Mary Grace, though Gordon still referred to her as Mary Grace.

Kathy also felt she was being avoided by "Mary Grace," and that was unacceptable. Not that Kathy had a thing about going after anyone. The truth was, her heart was big and compassionate, which could be testified to by the last stray cat she had brought home and foisted onto her patient, dog-loving husband, J.D. Webb. The evenly marked black and white male cat had an odd deformity in its throat that caused him to choke on regular cat food, which he had promptly done when he wolfed down the resident cat's dry food after Kathy left for work. That left the dog-loving J.D. to revive the limp cat. Which he did: with the "kiss" of life. Something he didn't much want to talk about.

From that day on Elroy followed J.D. like a dog. Even to mimicking J.D.'s posture as he stretched his long form out on the sofa where Kathy sometimes found them napping when she came home. J.D. had named the cat "Elroy" after his own father, who had hated the name Elroy and was pleased that his future bride had shortened the name to "El" when she met him. She hadn't like it either. But Cat Elroy came on the run when J.D. called him by it. And Kathy's pet-vet laughed at the name as he prescribed the special food for the cat whose life was saved when the Webb's took him in.

It had been a hot day, not unexpected near the end of August as Kathy patrolled about the city, an otherwise nicely quiet day. Soon she would be on her way home from her shift, ready for a relaxing glass of red wine with J.D., to talk over each other's day. Her husband was a lawyer, and sooner or later, met some of Kathy's "clients." As she passed "The Kitchen Sink," she saw the mysterious "Mary" entering the restaurant and made an instant decision to meet the woman. Pulling into a parking spot close by, Kathy walked nonchalantly back and into the restaurant, casually glancing around the busy room until she spotted Marti almost hidden by others waiting for a booth or stool. Not wanting to single the woman out in the crowd and having no intention of waiting to order a cup of coffee, she grinned at someone she recognized, shrugged her shoulders and left.

As she walked into her kitchen, J.D. was carrying two marinated steaks out to the grill, Elroy at his heels, and he had called out, "Twenty-five minutes." No more dwelling on "Mary." The woman wasn't breaking any laws, and there was no lawful reason to be investigating her.

DEL ROBERTSON

Marti was troubled by her fear of the policewoman who crossed her path so often. She had begun to feel "watched" by Officer Webb. She wondered if she should approach the officer and truthfully tell her she feared for her life at the hands of her husband. Perhaps Lucy could help her resolve this issue. Marti decided to bring it up at card night this week.

It had been a busy day at the nursing home with two new admissions. One had gone to the locked wing for those whose memories had left them. An elderly man had been admitted to her wing for therapy following surgery for a fractured hip. He hadn't been happy to have to be there but was at least cooperative. His wife had stayed as long as she could. But her exhaustion was obvious. As she left, she relayed to Marti her nephew was bringing a suitcase with clothes, personal items, and reading materials for her husband. The nephew hadn't arrived yet by the time her shift ended so she passed the word on to the next shift and clocked out.

She had passed through the second set of double doors and could see a man approaching carrying a suitcase and thought the nephew had arrived with his uncle's belongings. She had then put her cap over her hair and added the sunglasses, unaware the man had stopped a foot in front of her, and she would have gone on to her bicycle when hearing her name, "Marti!" stopped her in her tracks, making her heart lurch in her chest. Facing the man who had called out her name, she heard her own voice quavering as she answered, "Del? Del? Really?" And Del had set the suitcase down and in two steps, had wrapped his arms around her! She felt "blown-away."

He looked older, of course, and fine lines had formed near his eyes and mouth, showing strain; he looked more mature, thicker but yet looked almost the same. She wondered how he could have known her. She was thinner and her hat had been off. She knew her white hair altered her appearance significantly.

At one time their eyes and hair had matched so perfectly, and Del had been 5'7", considered short, so the two of them had been mistaken as brother and sister by friends and strangers. They used to laugh it off, but it had been annoying.

It had been memories of the Red Wing area, good memories, that had brought her there, and Del was part of that time. They had gone out together a few times the second summer she worked at the Bible camp, and Del had turned up. He had laughed as he said, "to check out the pretty waitresses." They had become friends and she had been impressed by how nice he was. He had even introduced her to his family, and she had liked all of them. But she had lived too far away for their friendship to develop into something more, and Del became a memory as "the nicest boy she knew." Not that she had dated all that much. She met Ted by the time she was eighteen—the worst of the worst.

She had not expected to see Del again, did not remember where he lived back then. She thought his parents had lived on a small farm, or maybe it was an acreage, outside a small town that she couldn't recall even being told the name of. After she returned home, there were one or two letters exchanged, then nothing. Each had gone their own way.

Now they were face-to-face, delighted at meeting again, but at a loss for words, from surprise. Marti didn't know what to say since there was nothing she could comfortably share. And Del, too, was not at ease with where things had gone awry in his life. All he could say with warmth and sincerity was, "I am so glad to see you again, Marti! How long have you worked here?" By her uniform, that much he had guessed. Her answer was much the same as what he had said to her, that it was good meeting him again after so many years. And that she had worked at the nursing home only a few months.

They had moved to let people by; some entering, others leaving, and Del had abruptly asked if she'd be free for a visit over coffee and lunch one day soon. Marti's hesitant response wasn't missed by Del, and he rushed into an apology, saying something about understanding if she'd rather not.

And Marti remembered she had been the one who wrote the last letter. Seeing the beginning signs of disappointment in his eyes, she swallowed her apprehension and answered, "It would be nice to have time to chat, Del. Perhaps sometime we can, but I lead a very dull life—I have no phone and my landlady allows no visitors."

By the last comment, Del felt certain Marti lived alone, either divorced or widowed.

"What is an eating place you like, Marti?"

Wanting to keep "The Kitchen Sink" free of entanglements

for herself, she named "Martin's Food Stand" in the small city park.

Del had asked when her next day off was, and a lunch date was made.

Marti had left feeling troubled and a little down. But Del had picked up his uncle's suitcase and strolled into the nursing home with a song in his heart.

Later, as he reached open highway outside city limits, Del let the unexpected meeting with Marti replay in his mind. He had always known he cared more for Marti than she had cared for him. He hadn't gotten over her last letter easily when she had ended their correspondence.

As soon as he graduated, he had joined the army. When he was a civilian again, he had attended a university for a while but couldn't settle in and went into a community college, training in auto mechanics. It hadn't been a bad choice; he had been able to buy and own his gas and service station within a few years, making a good living for his wife and their two sons, Neal and Jack. Gaye had been the bad choice of his life. It was over now. He didn't want to even think about her. He wondered why she had wanted to marry him, which she obviously had. She was bored by housework, hated cooking, never thought of laundry till she needed clean clothes. If she couldn't party on weekends, she was hell to be around during the week. The boys had numerous babysitters while he was at work. Gaye wouldn't stay home. Del didn't know who Jack's father was, but Del found it unacceptable to reject an innocent child and he treated and loved Jack as he did Neal. They were both "his" sons. Gaye he had divorced two years earlier, unable to tolerate her presence any longer, which he had been doing for the sake of the boys. Del had dreaded telling his parents of the divorce; they were devout in their faith and had always talked against divorce. He was surprised to find they were relieved Gaye would be out of their lives.

They had married when Gaye told Del she was pregnant.

They had eloped to Las Vegas to be married. On returning home and making the announcement to his parents, Del could still recall the sick looks on the faces of both his parents.

No. he wasn't proud of the choices he'd made. Providing for his sons was what Del worked for. He had turned the space over his repair shop into a two-bedroom apartment where the boys spent most of their time.

Gaye had gotten the house, alimony, and half-time with the boys, but wanting her freedom to enjoy herself, the boys would show up at Del's at odd times. Twelve-year-old Neal was interested in his father's work and knew how to change a bicycle tire among other things. Jack, eight years old, followed his older brother and father, interested in everything. They had their room over the garage where they were expected to do their homework under Del's watchful eyes. Where they had three square meals a day, and clean clothes.

When Del needed a babysitter, he called on his mother and his single sister, Jane.

The boys were supposed to be with their mother, but he was anxious to be back in case they had come back to the shop. He had hired a young mechanic as his repair work increased; and now had a dependable high school boy run the gas station till nine p.m. He kept the apartment locked when he had to be gone after he had surprised Gaye there when he had left it unlocked for the boys. She had been going through his personal papers. What followed had been an acrimonious exchange of angry words in front of the boys.

He had been planning to give Neal a housekey, but changed his mind knowing Gaye would get her hands on it--or make a copy. She had begun sending the boys' dirty laundry with them when they came to be with him. She wasn't using the child support money to buy new clothes for them either. She delivered them with outgrown shoes and clothes in their carryalls. He had reached the point where he could hardly bear the sight of her.

Marti planned to be in the park at least a few minutes before Del arrived, but he had arrived early and she had watched him as he walked to the bench nearest Martin's stand, where he seated himself. Rolo was a regular at that bench and Marti felt disturbed for Rolo. She hoped he would not see where she had come from; but all things considered, what did it matter? He would be asking where she lived, and she had decided to go with honest answers when asked. He may have already asked questions at her workplace.

As it turned out the presence of Rolo passing by him seated on the bench distracted Del and he missed seeing Marti leaving Fay's house across the street from the park and didn't see her until she was passing her own preferred bench. On seeing Marti, Del had risen and headed in her direction. Rolo had turned in his tracks and was instantly taking up residence on the bench he most favored.

Marti stopped and waited for Del to reach her, then turned towards the shaded seat sheltered by the trees and bushes, holding a hand out in the direction of the bench. She had moved away from him when it seemed he was about to hug her again, and seated herself, leaving ample room for Del. He hadn't missed anything. He wondered what had happened to her to have made her seem so closed off, or closed in. She was so changed.

Something was moving on the other side of Marti; and Del's eyes widened on what had followed Marti into the park.

"Ye gods—what's that?" Came from a disbelieving Del.

And Marti laughed heartily when she saw what he was focused on. "That's Mincemeat, Del. He's a legend in his own time. Let me tell you about him." And she gave him the history of the amazing cat--and in the process revealed where she lived. Somehow, she didn't care anymore. She was ready to talk. Lucy had helped prepare the way back for her.

Comfortably sitting together at the end of a beautiful September day in the peacefulness of the park, Marti and

Del slowly and thoughtfully began filling in the missing years since they first met. Marti felt again the goodness that seemed to emanate from Del; his genuine interest in everything she had to say, the warm kindness, and acceptance in his eyes and voice. She asked him questions about his life in the intervening years, and he had been open with his answers, making no excuses, asking for no sympathy for the choices he had made. The welfare and love of his two sons were foremost in his life now.

At a pause in their conversation, Del had suggested a coffee or cold drink from Martin's stand. Del pointed to Marti's dark glasses and asked—just for this afternoon, to take them off. She had hesitated at first, then folded and put them in a pocket. They had wandered over to order their drinks and look over Martin's menu to choose their lunch for later.

Martin had been watching with interest. He had liked Marti from the first day she came to his stand, but when she stood before him beside Del without her "shades," and he looked into two sets of the greenest eyes he had ever seen, he mistakenly believed the 5'7" Del and petite Marti were brother and sister.

When Del openly admired the attractive and unique food stand, Martin decided he liked Del, too. When Del said it was one-of-a-kind, Martin's face had fairly glowed.

They had walked slowly, with their coffee in hand, through the winding walks of the small park, their voices low, most times serious, occasional laughter. Rolo sat on his bench, lost in his own memories.

Del knew now what had brought Marti to Red Wing, and his anger at the foul Ted burned in him but was kept well-hidden. It was beyond his comprehension how a man could be so evil.

Their leisurely walk brought them back to the food stand where they put their pre-determined orders in.

When Marti placed a third order and brought out her

money for it, Del knew what she was doing and had covered her hand with his, and shaking his head had said, "I'll get this," and grinned knowingly at her.

Carrying their food, the pair ambled past Rolo warming himself in the sun, and Marti, barely pausing, held out the food to him with a smile. Accepting what was offered, Rolo looked up into Marti's eyes, and smiled. No one noticed Kathy driving slowly past, taking in the inviting scene that made her smile on the inside. Mincemeat had been ambling with the couple, knowing Marti would feed him.

It had been a good day for both Marti and Del. A healing day in a strange way. They had found a genuine friendship in each other. Mincemeat walked Marti back to her apartment, then disappeared through the hedge into Lucy's yard.

Before it got any later, Marti decided to make her run to the grocery for things she needed. Cleaning supplies, and foods that didn't need refrigeration. Her needs were few.

Kathy's day was ending when J.D. called her to ask if she minded picking up sour cream and green onions on her way home. He had added "and red wine." He was fixing what she knew would be so-o-o good for their evening meal. Kathy called him a "closet chef." He definitely had a magic touch with food. And her, she added. She had called him the "nicest human being she had ever met" to more than one acquaintance. Officer Webb loved her J.D. with all her heart.

It would be a quick stop for what J.D. wanted. No problem. She was hungry, as well as tired. It would be good to get home and kick her shoes off. Rounding an aisle, Kathy came face-to-face with the elusive "Mary-Marti" and this time, without dark glasses hiding half her face. Both stopped, momentarily confused. Looking into Marti's wide eyes, Kathy saw despair, and a resigned sadness. She had nodded to the pale-faced woman, then pleasantly greeted her saying, "I hope you like Red

Wing. It's a good place to be," and passed on by, but heard the soft, "Thank you, Officer." The one thing Kathy knew for sure was that Mary-Marti was more likely to be a victim than a miscreant.

Over the next few days when Kathy found the time that a search could require, she periodically looked into any available means to find where Marti had come from. Nothing turned up in Minnesota, but a Martha Gracek, from a small town north of Des Moines, had a driver's license about twenty years ago, but none since. That didn't mean she couldn't have had them in other states. Instead of wasting any more time going down that rabbit hole, Kathy began searching marriage licenses in Iowa and eventually found one for Martha Gracek and Theodore Sweltzer, dated almost twenty years ago, too. Was Marti a runaway wife? That was a possible explanation. But why was she afraid of police? Something felt wrong. Had she done something to her husband?

Kathy began to research the name Theodore Sweltzer and there she stumbled onto the Des Moines police reports of the attempted abduction of his wife, Martha. From that time, she went missing for three years until last May when it became known she was in Decorah, Iowa but had again disappeared after a break-in at her apartment. Police had questioned the husband. No arrests made at this time.

Kathy slumped back in her chair as she looked down at the pile of papers, she had been amassing for almost a month. Her instinct told her "spousal abuse." Maybe this husband preferred the wife dead? Kathy believed that was exactly what Marti feared. The name of Officer Tate Osbourn came to Kathy's attention, but it would be a mistake to draw attention to Marti at this point.

Gathering up what looked like a lot of evidence, but which merely held only scraps of relevant details, Kathy put it in a locked drawer in her desk. There was nothing she could do but a gut instinct told her, "Something wicked this way comes."

As she and J.D. relaxed in front of their fireplace, digesting another of J.D.'s gourmet specialties, she told him all she knew of the Martha and Theodore Sweltzer case, and he had listened intently, getting up once to refill their wine glasses. She waited as he thought through what she had uncovered. He agreed with what she believed about Sweltzer but added there was nothing to be done at this point. If Sweltzer was as bad as what he appeared to be, it was only a matter of time before he would sniff his prey out again. It was at this point J.D had aimed a stern look in his wife's direction and told her, "Don't even think about involving yourself in this. You know how that would go over with Des Moines police! Don't. Even. Think it!" How well he knew her. She was itching to go after Sweltzer.

Marti had left the grocery store unsure of what she was feeling, or what to make of the female officer. Her mind still hadn't settled down by the time she got home, but she remained constantly aware of everything around her, listening in the dimness where she parked her bike, and she wished the light bulb was higher wattage. With winter coming she would begin leaving her bike in Lucy's old garage out on the alley and walk to work. It wasn't that far. She didn't like the dim light on the stairs to the third floor either. She would ask Gordon to "sound out" his grandmother about better lighting. She had turned her light bulb on when she went out so as to not walk into total darkness on her return. She tested the door latch, and finding it locked inserted the large key, unlocking it. Once inside, the process reversed, and the door was re-locked, and the old cane-less chair was pulled snugly under the iron latch. Sometimes she felt exhausted by the constant waiting for what had come to feel inevitable. Ted.

She put her few purchases away, then sat tiredly down on the one chair at her table and rested her head on her forearms.

Perhaps it was time to ask for help from the police. Ted wasn't friends with anyone on the Red Wing force. Maybe they would listen. The policewoman had seemed so nice and kind. Marti thought perhaps that should be who she talked to.

She wanted to be free of the rock. She had become afraid to not have the rock with her at all times; needing to feel it in her pocket, thinking of it as a lucky charm. And she couldn't sleep without her fingers on it under her pillow at night. The only time she felt safe was when she was with Lucy. During the last time they had played cards, Lucy had encouraged Marti to change her routine; she had laughingly said people could set their clocks by Marti's coming and going. That was when Lucy offered the garage to store her bike.

PROVERBS 21:26
"All day long the wicked covets…"

Gaye was angry. And upset. And most of all jealous. She had been full of disbelief when Del served her with divorce papers, and she had used all her wiles to get him to change his mind. She couldn't believe it when that failed; and then she did all she could to make everything as difficult and costly as she could for him. She had convinced herself everything was his fault. He had to have been seeing another woman somewhere. Gaye just hadn't been able to find out who--or where—but not for lack of trying.

She had enjoyed her easy life married to Del. It wasn't as good since the divorce and, she not only wanted things back the way they were, but she also believed in her ability to make it so.

She had at last caught Del meeting with his "tramp." This was when the jealousy had kicked in. In the past, as Gaye tracked him, Del had always seemed his usual pleasant self. This time Gaye couldn't miss how happy Del had become. He'd bought new clothes and went oftener for haircuts. Now he was meeting the slut every week in a park in Red Wing, while his mother stayed with the boys. Her jealousy grew by leaps and bounds. She had begun following Marti, learning where she worked, and had even gone into the nursing home, stood next to her at the nurses' station, pretending to wait for someone who was meeting her there. She had observed that she was close in size to Marti but wondered why in the world she didn't do something with her horrible hair. "Like, color it, for god's sake," was Gaye's recurring thoughts on Marti's hair. Gaye considered her own features and attributes to be far superior of other women, but especially so of the timid, color-less ____," and in her mind she came up with a string of derogatory descriptions.

On one of the days of following Del, Gaye had observed Marti coming down the stairs of the house across the street from the park where Del had been waiting on a bench, and she wondered, "Which apartment had she come from?" So, Gaye had returned one evening as lights were being turned on in windows up and down the street. In the second level tower room window a light came on and for a brief moment Gaye glimpsed an old man. Ah! One down, two to go, and she concentrated on watching the third level tower room window. After several puzzling minutes she was sure there was a dim glow from somewhere within.

As she watched, Marti arrived on her bike which she parked in the shadows beneath the stairs. Carrying a sack, she had entered an unlocked door on the landing. Watching the dim light on the top level, a shadow had moved across the window once. Gaye rose from the bench and walked past the house until she could see the windows of the entire second level. No lights were on in the back half of the level. Totally dark. Gaye left feeling confident she knew where Marti's apartment was.

PROVERBS 5:22

"His own wrongdoings will trap the wicked..."

Leaving his father well cared for over the next few days, Ted left his own car parked in his father's driveway and took a taxi to a car rental. Then was quickly on his way to Red Wing. He believed it would not be difficult tracking Martha. She was so predictable, and the city was not that big. Ted's mood fairly soared; he felt exhilarated, excited. The miles flew by and the rental was quite comfortable. Armed with maps of Iowa and Minnesota, he looked for the best route to Red Wing, opting to go through Rochester instead of Faribault when roadwork signs warned of detours ahead.

Ted was oblivious of the small towns and "burgs" scattered between forest and farmland. It was beautiful country, becoming more pine tree forested, with bridges over many streams. The highway wound through heavy forest, up and down hills, sometimes cutting through rock. The beauty of the scenery was lost on Ted.

By the time he reached Red Wing, he was stiff from sitting and low on gas. Pulling into the first station he saw, his good mood had slipped considerably but already he was looking around, his eyes drawn to any small woman. He already knew how she had changed her appearance, and her choice of disguise. So predictable. What a drag. By now she must have spent, or wasted, the small fortune she'd stolen from him. That memory had instantly enraged him, and he had slammed both fists with all his force against the steering wheel. Mentally cursing her, he got out and began filling the gas tank. A teenager, the passenger of a car in the next bay had been casually watching Ted as he waited for the driver to return, and was startled by the violence he witnessed. As the driver returned and opened the car door, the boy spoke. "Wow! Wonder what go under that guy's skin!? He almost broke his steering wheel, Dad."

"What, Gord? What'd you say?" Then he started his car and they drove off.

Ted couldn't resist driving slowly down Main Street, making note of the eating places, and reminded himself mentally to be sure to look for a bike parked in front of those places. If he saw a bike, he'd park and watch to see who claimed it. If it was Martha, Ted would follow her to where she was living. Just imagining such success filled him with euphoria. Then he took himself off to a motel on the edge of town to make sure he had a place to sleep before going out to eat.

He had learned a lot about how Martha had lived for the three years she had escaped notice. He had bribed Archie to give him all the information in the police files and he now had most of the details of her life in Decorah. Ted knew she cleaned houses, got clothes from a Methodist church, got around on a bike, and spent her free time in a park or a library. And that she hid behind dark glasses and a cap. Oh, he *really* knew her so well! He had a story ready that he was looking for a good housekeeper for his "sickly wife," when he would be questioning the hicks in these "backwoods." And, during the meal hours, he would be looking for a bike parked in front of restaurants. If this god-forsaken place had a park, he'd find it; thus went his thoughts and, with those plans in mind, Ted retired to his room and looked through the phonebook for churches, restaurants, and parks.

Morning dawned with a cold drizzle of rain, infuriating Ted. This would put a damper on Martha biking out to eat. Same thing for the only park he had found in the phonebook. Still, he had made a few random passes past the eating places and had finally gone into Ed's Eatery for his own breakfast after a pointless cruise around what passed as a park for the local "yokels." At least the drizzle had thinned out the customers, and he had a booth to himself. And the food was good. At the décor he mentally sneered. The bell jingled frequently, and he always glanced up just in case Martha had walked out for her breakfast. This he did not want. He didn't want her aware he was in town. At the next jingle, he looked up to see a female police officer enter. That was one more unacceptable thing for Ted. Women needed to know their place, and that was not to be taking over men's jobs or giving orders to anyone. It still rankled in Ted to have been pulled over for speeding by a female cop years ago. When the opportunity had presented itself, he had slashed one of her patrol car's tires. He despised female cops.

Ted could hear "Ed" greeting the woman by her first name and paused in eating his breakfast to watch. They appeared to be friends and mutually respectful, talking over politics and the upcoming election on November 6th. Jimmy Carter, with his theme of "Why Not the Best?" was running against Gerald Ford. The officer got a coffee to-go, leaving money on the counter to cover it, reminded Ed to vote, and left as Ted stood and prepared to pay for his order. At the register, he put on his "charm" act for the owner as he fished for information on a good housekeeper for the fictional "sickly wife." Ed said he was sorry, but he didn't know anyone who cleaned houses. Using a regretful tone of voice, Ted mentioned he had heard of someone named Martha who had sounded well-recommended. Had Ed heard of her by any chance? Once again, the answer had been, "No." What a wasted morning.

Ted had followed his plan throughout the dreary day, driving past the places of business where Martha was likely to go, as well as around the park several times. By the time he turned in for the night, Ted was in a foul mood.

Day Two seemed a repeat of Day One, but Day Three dawned clear with the promise of a rare last day to be enjoyed outdoors. Ted made passes past the diners with no bike sighted.

Mid-afternoon, Ted had parked the rental a block away and casually walked into the park. He had added a hat and trench coat, not wanting to be recognized should Martha come by. A bum in an old army coat lay stretched on a bench in the sun, while an older man busily worked on some sort of food stand. It was shuttered; apparently, the old guy was shutting it down until Spring, winterizing it. Ted had come even with the bum on the bench, and he gave in to his frustration in a burst of anger and slammed a foot into the bench while at the same time snarling at the unsuspecting man, "Get!! Get outta here! Now! You---" and what followed was a string of filthy words. And the stunned man had nearly fallen as he scrambled to flee.

Shouts of "Hey-you! Stop that! Stop it, right now—no need for that!"

Startled, Ted saw the old man trying to run towards him

and Ted turned on him, shouting back, "Back off, you old fool! Get!" And the man had answered, "I will, and I'll be back with the police. Come on, Rolo." And Martin began to rush back, past the closed-up food stand and across the street to what apparently was his home where he could phone the police.

By the time Kathy arrived, Ted had disappeared through the park to where he could get into his car without being seen.

But someone had watched everything with chilling clarity.

Kathy had questioned Martin and Rolo, getting a description of the man who had behaved violently. He didn't fit anyone she knew. Driving around the neighborhood turned up nothing.

Ted was furious with himself. He hadn't intended to draw attention to himself and now he feared someone may have noticed his car! Damn! Three days wasted! Changes in his plan would need to be made. It meant returning the rental for one that looked completely different. He spent the rest of the day in his motel room. He had one thing to do before leaving after dark.

That night, Martin's Food Stand burned to the ground. The fire had been deliberately set by someone who had poured combustible fluid around the entire base of the structure and then tossed a match on it. Martin stood weeping in the street. It was all he had left of his son, an only child. A son who had designed, planned, and built the stand as a teenage school project with his father's help. He had been drafted after graduation, and then became MIA.

Ted slipped out of Red Wing during the dark of night, satisfied that one score had been settled. Still not having Martha in his sights, and now with no follow-up plan, Ted's stomach was churning with acid. He was agitated but drove within the speed limit. Getting stopped by a cop was the last thing he wanted or needed. Passing through a small burg, his headlights swept over the sign of a darkened gas station, "Del's Repair and Gas," and it took several seconds before the name registered in Ted's memory and as soon as it did, his foot came off the gas and he slowed until he could turn the car around to make another pass by the business. Once more he turned, passing slowly while a new plan formed in his mind. With hope returning, Ted became calmer, and he continued on to Rochester where he found a motel for the rest of the night, sleeping in late the next morning.

Turning in the rental car, he then found a competitor rental company and was finally back on the road, heading back to Red Wing, but planning on a stop at "Del's Repair" first. As he neared the small town, Ted pulled into a sheltered area and let enough air out of a tire to necessitate a stop at the next gas station. Del's. And now Del's was open with a teenage boy behind the cash register in the small office area. Ted pulled up in a parking space and then casually walked towards the repair bay where two men worked under a car raised on a hydraulic lift over a pit.

Ted was an expert at "schmoozing" as he called it, which is what made him such a good salesman. Now he approached the two grease-covered mechanics with his perfect "good guy," so-friendly "persona" on his handsome face. No one would have ever guessed all that was hidden behind that smiling demeanor.

Both men looked up at the stranger coming towards them, but it was the older of the two who greeted Ted pleasantly, asking if he could help him. Ted apologized for having to bother them; probably all about nothing anyway, but well, you know...when nature calls (ha-ha)—anyway, as he was getting back in the car, he'd spotted the low tire. Boy! You never know what you're getting when you rent a car.

And so, it went: "Saw your sign—either of you Del?"

The older man had smiled and said, "I'm Del. Let's take a look at that tire."

Ted had already known he was looking at the Del from the old photo from Martha's album, and his fingers had clenched into fists while he continued to smile and chat up the "grease monkeys." Ted wanted to beat in the face of the smaller man. He knew he'd have no problem doing it, but there were more important things to be dealt with first. This could wait till later.

Del had thoroughly checked the tire, discerning no punctures, no leaks, and had re-inflated Ted's tire at no charge. Ted left, still wanting to beat Del to a pulp. But if Martha was seeing her old boyfriend again, then it was *sine qua non* for Ted to watch and follow him straight to the ... (once again, Ted mentally unleashed his extensive, disgusting vocabulary.)

Looking over the cars parked at the station as Del checked the tire over, Ted had guessed the newest car belonged to Del when two young boys had appeared and called him "Dad." The two "beaters" belonged to the hired help, it would appear.

Now the following and watching would begin, leading him to the tramp—the sooner, the better!

Ted chose to register in a motel on the edge of Red Wing, close on the highway where incoming traffic was more visible.

The following day, he had driven past Del's station several times and the newer-looking blue car hadn't moved. The waiting was torture to Ted. He realized the waiting could involve several days, and with each day the risk of being noticed increased. And then, by a fluke, as he drove into a fast-food for an early evening sandwich--two days after the tire episode, Ted saw Del driving past, and Ted left the line in a hurry, getting out into the traffic, weaving in and out, keeping the blue car in sight, slowly gaining on it until it pulled in near the park he had been in a few nights earlier. He could feel a fine film of sweat on his face, but he had slowly passed, then turned, circling the block and parking one street over; walking unhurriedly, had casually entered one of the park paths, staying closer to evergreens and the large trunks of old trees until Del was visible on a bench further into the park. He was obviously waiting for someone, and Ted had no doubt that "someone" was the object of his long, dragged-out pursuit. Locating a bench affording himself a good view of the area Del appeared to be glancing up at, Ted unfolded the newspaper he had picked up a couple days earlier which he'd discarded in the car. Now he looked like a gentleman enjoying one of the last good outdoor days, relaxing while catching up with news. So bucolic. He studied the large Victorian homes over the top of the newspaper, noting the stairs added to the side of the house on the corner, and had felt an odd prickling of the skin of his arms. The hunter had found the rabbit's "hidey-hole." And Martha—the punctual, as if he had conjured her up, was descending the steps. How well he knew her. He also knew her dog from hell was back in Decorah. That would be dealt with after Martha. And Del.

Folding the paper, Ted-the-Triumphant, walked lightly back to his car, unaware of the eyes burning into his back; nor did he see the evergreen branch in front of him slowly slide back into place. Ted was pre-occupied with planning the punishment Martha so richly deserved.

Tomorrow he'd be watching her coming and going. He had to know more about her schedule, which apartment. And he wanted enough time to make her wish she'd never been born.

The nice days ended abruptly. Ted was up very early, eager to begin spying on his prey. He knew she must have found employment and he needed to know her hours, but with the drop in temperature and the cold wind he would not be sitting in the park. He needed to park close enough to watch, but far enough to be of no interest.

He'd nearly missed her as he looked around to park advantageously, and suddenly seen her pedaling out into the street, turning to the right. And he had followed her to a nursing home, of all things, where she locked her bike to a stand and entered the building.

When she hadn't come out by noon, he had no doubt she worked the day shift, and he then had a general idea of when she would be returning to her apartment. And he planned to be there to welcome her.

REST HOME

At the nurses' station, the charge nurse picked up the phone on the second ring, and as she listened to the caller she wrote on a notepad, ending with, "I'll give her your message, Mrs. Radstone." She had continued with her nurse's notes as she neared the end of her shift but kept an eye on each person passing her desk. She knew Marti would be coming by any moment, but the nurse had to be ready before three p.m. with her report, so she didn't track down Marti with the message: and nearly missed delivering the missive. As she hurried to the report room, she saw Marti clocking-out, and urgently called to her, pulling the note out of her pocket and waving it in the aide's direction.

Marti read the note for the third time in a mixture of

puzzlement and uneasiness. Why did Lucy ask her to please call her before she left her workplace? And she had added: "Important." Marti used the phone at the nurses' station to make the call. With the charge nurse making her shift change report, the phone was conveniently available. And private.

Marti was still puzzled as she rode her bike towards home with her head down, leaning into a cold wind, but she followed Lucy's requests and went home using a slightly different route; then she pedaled down the alley to Lucy's garage where she stored her bike, and used the garden path to Lucy's back door. The enclosed porch was unlocked for her, but she locked it behind herself and knocked on the aged kitchen door. Fern let Marti in, telling her Lucy was in the living room. Fern was unnaturally quiet.

The drapes in the living room were closed, and soft light glowed from several silk shaded lamps. Daylight was getting shorter, and it had been a gloomy day as well, but in Lucy's living room it was warm and pleasant. Lucy was seated in the curtained alcove with the low light from the lamp shadowing a "sunkenness" about her face, and Marti felt a moment of disbelief as she realized fully that Lucy wasn't just a frail woman, she was an extremely sick woman.

Her steps grew slower the closer she came to her friend, and words failed her completely.

"Don't look like that, Marti. I've known for a long time. And I'm fine with it. What we must talk about is you, my dear. Sit down, and please listen to me. I do know what you are going through. You know already my first husband was an abusive man, and like yours, could not let me go." Lucy's voice was weak, and she paused frequently for breath. Her eyes seemed to be looking into the past.

"Such a long time ago," sounded sad. Moments passed and Lucy was again focused on Marti. "You will stay here tonight—please, don't argue. And you will be calling in sick for the next few days. Do you understand what I'm telling you? I believe your husband has found you."

Marti lost her breath, grew weak, and slumped into the soft chair, her head rolling back and forth, and she heard a voice moaning— "no—no—no---," her own voice.

A cold, wet cloth was on her forehead and Fern's kind face hovered into Marti's vision, "Take some deep breaths, you'll be okay in a few minutes."

Marti had come around but resisted believing Ted could have found her in only a few months. It couldn't be true! It couldn't!

"Some men never give up until they kill you. Your husband seems so much like mine was. It's time to involve the police, Marti."

"No! Lucy, you know they do nothing until it's too late. Even you are not safe as long as you try to help me. I must leave! Right away! I'm so tired!"

Fern had placed a box of tissues on Marti's lap, and she was constantly wiping her face. "I don't know what to do any-more. I just don't—oh, Lucy! How did you escape!?" Seconds ticked by, and for the first time, Marti was aware of the man-tle clock over the fireplace "ticking" steadily in the silence of the room, and Lucy was so motionless, Marti wondered if she were breathing. Then clearly, sadly, Marti heard her say, "I killed him. Accidentally, but none-the-less, *I killed him*. With a heavy skillet as he came at me."

In low voices, interspersed with long silences, the two women talked over everything.

Lucy asked Marti to describe Ted. As she finished, Lucy slow-ly nodded her head and then told her all she had witnessed from her chair in the alcove through the binoculars she had taken to using when she could no longer get out to the park. She had ob-served Martin lovingly preparing the unique food stand for the winter weather as he did each year. Asking Marti if she knew the history of it, she had shaken her head. Lucy's eyes grew sad as she continued, "I knew Martin's son when he was in high school.

That stand was Matthew's school project. He drew up the plans, designed it, he was exceptionally talented, and Martin encouraged him from the beginning. Matt was an only child. The project was outstanding, and Matt and Martin had quite a little business together, but when Matt was drafted, they put it in storage. Matt never came home. Missing in Action. Martin has set it up every year since. I think it made him feel close to his son." It had been a long discourse for Lucy, and she leaned her head against her chair's head rest and closed her eyes.

Without opening her eyes, she continued, "I didn't see Martin's stand burn, but I have no doubt whatsoever Ted set fire to it. Lucy had gone on to say she believed it was Ted she had seen in the park the day Martin winterized his son's stand. She hadn't thought much about people wandering the park earlier but had picked up her binoculars when she had seen the tall, well-built man kick the bench Rolo lay on. She had been shocked, then mesmerized, by the swift interaction between Martin and the stranger. She had clear close-up looks at a handsome, light-eyed man, with a glimpse of blond hair around the edges of the hat he wore. His facial expression aimed at Martin was hate-filled. Lucy had experienced an awfully bad premonition.

Fern was beginning to watch Lucy anxiously. She had brought in sandwiches and a delicious fruit salad on trays and poured up coffee for the two women. Lucy was looking wan and tired, but also aware of Fern's concern, and reminded her friend it was too soon to turn in for the night. Besides, she wanted to watch the first snowfall while Marti was shown to a room for her use; and some time alone to think.

"If you would just put most of the lights out—leave one wall sconce, please. Yes, that's adequate. And if you would, open the drapes? Thank you, Fern."

Marti agreed to stay with Lucy, thanking her gratefully, but also knowing she really had no choice. But she still wanted no police involvement. At least not yet. She needed more time to think things over longer.

CHRIS & GULLY

Almost four months had passed, and no one knew anything more about Marti's whereabouts. Chris had used the time to befriend Gulliver. The dog appeared to have benefitted under the advice and guidance of a man--an ex-G.I., a veterinarian had recommended to work with traumatized dogs, helping them to cope. Gulliver trusted Chris enough now to allow him to stroke his ears.

He was working now on getting the dog to go with him in the car. Gully would follow Chris to the car when he left for errands or needed to check up on his property. It was obvious the dog was stressed whenever Chris left. Gilbert had reported that Gully would check frequently where he had last seen Chris and was always waiting by the time he had pulled his car into its usual spot. But no matter the coaxing, the dog remained well outside and away from the open car door.

Until---the day Chris brought home the hamburgers from a fast-food. He had bought two burgers with fries, planning on sharing with Gulliver, who was waiting for him as he drove in. They had eaten together, with Chris seated on a bench he had made from scraps and placed outside his office door. He always kept food and water there for the shy dog. Now they ate burgers, side-by-side like two old friends. Chris had discovered Gully loved fast-food hamburgers! As well as fries. When Gully belched loudly after inhaling his food, Chris had laughed out loud.

Later he had opened all the car doors and begun cleaning the interior. Chris admitted he didn't keep a tidy car, but periodically did take a trash bag and clean it out. As he cleared the back seat area, he spotted the top of Gully's head as he sniffed the passenger seat where Chris had earlier placed the sack with burgers, driving home. The next day he again went to a fast-food, but on returning had stayed in the driver's seat, reaching over to swing open the passenger door. Opening the sack of warm food, the smell was mouthwatering, and Chris unwrapped one sandwich, placing it on the floormat. Then he had leaned back in his seat, opening the remaining sandwich for himself, and waited, eating slowly; ready to share his portion with the one who gulped his food without chewing. Patience and hamburgers won the day. Gully decided the car was okay after all.

The day came when the two of them would go to McDonald's drive-though, get their burgers and fries, and eat in the parking lot. The day Chris poured part of his shake into a Styrofoam bowl for Gully was when the dog overcame all dislikes of the car. And Chris laughed out loud once more as the dog licked the dish all the way home. Gilbert and Thora had watched the transformation with delight.

Another two months had passed, and Chris wondered if

this was the way it was going to be, and to just accept it. He had carried Henry's old rocker down below the balcony to where he and Gulliver sat to eat together if the weather permitted. The rocker was more comfortable than the hard bench. Gully liked being in the woodshop most of the time with Chris but wanted out when it got noisy.

The day had been one of dejection for Chris and he had become irritable and restless. He had not completed any of several orders he had waiting. When the phone rang, he expected it was a client checking in on an order, so it was with reluctance he picked it up. When he recognized the voice of Marti's mother on the line, he felt an electrifying jolt of energy and hope.

"Nancy! Hi! How are you? Got any good news?" He couldn't keep from going straight to word of Marti.

"I wish I could say 'yes', Chris--but, 'no.' Nothing has come to the attention of the police. I keep checking with them, but..." her voice trailed off for a few moments. "What I'm calling about may be meaningless—or maybe it could help. I was going through boxes of old photos. I was always going to organize them into albums, but I never got around to it. That was something Marti was good at. Anyway, I found pictures of her from a time I remember she was so happy. She loved working at a Bible camp outside Red Wing, Minnesota. She even dated a nice boy there the second year; she said it was the nicest place in the world. I've been wondering if maybe she's run back to a place she was happy.

Chris instantly knew he was going to be on his way to Minnesota as soon as he dealt with some phone calls and threw some clothes into a suitcase and gassed up the car! He literally ran to the Iversons to fill them in on his plans. Happiness glowed on the faces of the devoted couple as they already anticipated Chris would find their sweet Marti. As he turned to leave, he found Gulliver waiting behind him and it had brought him to a standstill. The dog was watching intently, and Chris's mind was racing. Then he spoke softly to the dog, "Come on, boy. Let's go."

Chris was studying the dog as he automatically locked his office door. He had called his clients to extend the expected delivery on their orders. Some were less happy than others, but none were pleased.

Now he made a fast trip up the steps to Marti's place, letting himself in with a key Gilbert had given him. He rummaged around until he located a large trash bag, then carefully placed the wrapped violin into the sack. He wanted Gully with him and hoped the familiar scent of Marti would have a calming effect should it be needed. Then he was on his way to the car with Gully awkwardly trying to keep up. Opening the passenger door, Chris placed the sack on the floormat leaving as much room as he could for the dog to climb in. Hesitant, Gully eased his nose to the sack, smelling its scent for what seemed like a long time to Chris, then hauled himself in, and up onto the seat and waited for Chris.

The hope filling his mind was, if the dog could find its way to the barn when Marti rode her bike from the park three years earlier, there just might be a chance he would pick up her scent in Red Wing. If she was there.

It had been an unusually warm Fall with several cold nights, but no hard freeze, so the greens of summer had turned the many shades of gold, red, yellow, and bronze. In other circumstances, Chris would have enjoyed the passing scenes, but a pervasive sense of urgency occupied his thoughts. He would have driven with no stops, except for gas, but he was concerned over the amount of stress for Gully, so he deliberately made two stops at Golden Arches he spotted, buying a burger at one, and a shake at the second, and was amazed at what looked like dog joy from Gully. By the time Red Wing came into view, it was late and finding a room took precedence, though once that was done, he drove around the city acquainting himself with it, trying to figure out what the best plan would be for the next day. He passed the police station and wondered about a stop there.

A policewoman was pulling out of the parking area lining one side of an old, but well-maintained brick building; and had waited for him to pass, her dark eyes following, noting the Iowa license plate, the good-looking man behind the steering wheel: clear, in the well-lit streets.

Back at the motel where he had requested a room where streetlights wouldn't keep him awake, he'd been directed to the far side of the business, where he then sneaked Gully into the room along with a bag of dog food, a leather chew bone and two dog bowls. An icy wind had come in from the north.

PROVERBS 26:27

"Whoever digs a pit will fall into it."

The wind was unpleasantly cold, a forerunner of the winter weather to come. The sun came and went, changing rapidly as clouds scudded across the sky, and Gaye sat in her car going over in her mind the plans that had been coming together for weeks.

Del had rebuffed her advances one time too many. She knew if she could drive off the competition, Del would get over the attraction, and eventually she would have him back. That's the way it always was.

She had concealed her hair under a warm winter hat and dressed in clothes resembling Marti's dull taste. Gaye knew the tramp's schedule; and Gaye's brother had put her in touch with a friend of his who had not only supplied her with lock-picks but had shown her how to pick a variety of locks. She was nothing if not well-prepared. The boys were with Del again. He got them to school and picked them up.

She parked the car on a side street where it was out of sight and knowing that occasionally Marti returned home through the alley, leaving her bike somewhere in the back yard and walking to the stairs, that's the way Gaye went now. So simple. On up the wooden steps and through the unlocked outer door, walking as quietly as she could, in case someone would wonder why Marti was home early. "It was good a light was on at the third-floor landing," was Gaye's thought as she got out the pick and set to work.

Easy work. Her brother's friend had taught her well. Once inside the apartment, Gaye took her time looking at everything, going into anything that could be opened. The fact that Marti had so little, the bare minimum for living, baffled Gaye. Nothing that was personally revealing could be found. The woman was a mystery, in a way, but as she thought more about her, Gaye judged Marti according to her own low standards and motivations. She believed Marti was after someone to support and take care of her. Someone to buy her whatever she wanted. Nothing but a gold-digger. Well! Gaye intended to put an end to that!

JOB 22:10

"Therefore traps surround you, and sudden dread terrifies you..."

Marti would be getting off work in another hour and Ted planned to "welcome" her home. He was glad it had been a dreary day, cold and windy. It had kept people indoors. He had dressed in dark clothing, with a winter hat, and was determined to make himself un-noticeable. His car was on a side street, near but out of sight. He didn't loiter in the chill wind but was business-like in his walk; cutting through the silent park and across the street, swiftly noting two mailboxes at the stair base bearing the names of two men—Level Two, which momentarily disconcerted him but then, swiftly, he was up the steps and through the unlocked door.

A quick look down the hall revealed three doors—once more messing with his expectations. Listening at the first door, he detected no sounds. Carefully turning the knob, he knew it was unlocked, and opening the door a mere sliver he knew it was a bathroom. He made no sound approaching the next door; again, heard no sound or movement within, and found the door locked. As he came near the last door, a tv could be heard, and someone sneezed explosively inside the apartment and Ted retreated soundlessly back down the hall to the end where the narrow steps could be seen.

As he looked upward, he shook his head, holding in a laugh—the attic? Did she live in an attic?

Still maintaining absolute quiet, he opened his lock-pick case, about to work on the door lock when he realized it was already unlocked, and again he almost laughed. How nice of her! He walked in, looking in disgust at the bare, dimly lit attic his wife had chosen to subsist in. It was then he heard someone in what Ted discerned as the bathroom, and he froze! She was home already? A day off? Home sick? What the hell? But so what!—he finally had her! He reached the open bathroom doorway as she came out. He instantly had his hands around her throat to stifle any screams—he wanted no attention from anyone else.

Her hands had flown up to ward him off, her mouth opened for a scream that never came; her hat had fallen from her head and Ted saw black hair and a face he didn't know. A face contorted with terror, her long red fingernails clawing at the hands squeezing her throat. She struggled, all for nothing.

Ted was in a fury. He killed her. What had gone wrong? Who was this bitch? He'd been absolutely sure this was Martha's hideout. He left the body where he dropped it and began the search for evidence this was indeed where Martha lived. A black permanent marker lay on the floor by the bathroom door, and ugly writing intended to scare Martha was scrawled randomly around the small bathroom. Ted realized he had crossed paths with Del's jealous wife. "Well, wasn't that just too bad!" His rage had diminished when he realized why the woman was there. She had dropped a can of spray paint when he had surprised her.

Ted seated himself on the one chair at the table and proceeded to wait for Martha to show up from work. He looked at his watch in anticipation. Thirty minutes passed, and he fidgeted. When an hour had passed and Martha hadn't shown up, he began pacing, looking out the tower windows into a darkening day. What had he missed? He had watched from his car the day before after seeing her come down the steps. He had seen her return following her "date" in the park. He had come early enough to see her come out before seven a.m. and leave for the nursing home. He knew he had found her apartment. So, what had gone wrong? She should have returned. Was she running errands?

Back at the window again he could see a haze in the air, and he realized it was snow. He didn't mind—it made better cover for him, but he decided to wait longer. She may have had to work late or run some errand. Hours passed. It was dark outside except for the fuzzy glow of a streetlamp; the fine snow was still blowing. In the dim light of the single bulb Martha had left turned on, Ted paced with increasing fury. She had to have seen him and was on the run again!

He rushed from the attic apartment, not caring if anyone heard him.

Down the steps, across the street, cursing as his feet slipped in a film of snow. He turned his head to glare up at the faint glow in the tower room window. He didn't hear anything with the wind soughing in the pine trees, and turning back, he had a flash of shock to be confronted by a figure in heavy winter clothing who made one upward thrusting motion into Ted's chest. He felt as though he had been hit hard with a fist, and staggered sideways, turning slowly, and felt the bench seat at the backs of his legs. His mouth had opened but no sound came out. In disbelief he felt himself falling, onto the bench, no feeling in his legs, no feeling---. The dark figure leaned over him, watching in the dim light for several minutes. Reaching out a gloved hand to the still form on the bench, the figure withdrew something from Ted's chest as the swirling snow melted on the upturned face and open eyes.

The dark-cloaked figure walked the park path to the sidewalk along the street, then bending over at the sidewalk edge forced something straight down into the yet unfrozen ground using a heel to plunge it in further.

In the kitchen, Fern heard the tinkle of the handbell which was always within Lucy's reach these days; and wiping her hands on a towel where she had been finishing cleaning up the pots and pans from the dinner preparation, she headed for the living room where Lucy and Marti would talk further and, perhaps, have a game of cards.

"Why in the world are you sitting in the dark?" Fern's voice held the hint of a scold, as she entered the essentially dark room and began turning lights on.

"Would you pull the drapes, please, Fern? There's a coldness coming from the windows."

"And yet, here you sit just inviting a cold! Why didn't you call sooner?" Fern genuinely cared about Lucy's well-being, and dreaded what she knew was coming for Lucy.

"You are a dear, Fern. What would I do without you? Do you know if Marti will be down soon?"

"I think she will be. The shower shut off a while ago. Do you want the fireplace lit?"

"Yes. That would feel so good! We'll have the card table there—and a glass of sherry, maybe?"—and Lucy gave a soft laugh.

With everything in place as Lucy wanted, Fern helped the

frail woman up from the chair by the now-draped windows and walked with her across the room to a chair close to the cheerful fire. Lucy sank down into it, accepting a soft shawl over her knees, giving a gentle stroke to Fern's hand.

Marti entered as Fern left, giving Marti a concerned and questioning look. "Seems like Lucy's determined to have a game of cards, Marti...and a little sherry." With that said, Fern headed back to the pots and pans, still waiting in the sink. Lucy had taught Marti several card games during the time they met for cards and fellowship.

The clock on the mantel would soon chime another hour passed. The two figures had been dealing and playing cards, mixed with quiet conversation until Lucy sat back in the comfortable armchair, holding her empty wine glass in one hand.

"Have you decided yet about making that phone call to the police, Marti? I do recommend it, my dear."

"I know. I know," was the despairing response." I can't run anymore. And I cannot stay here forever." More minutes ticked by before Marti added in a resigned voice, "I will call that policewoman tomorrow. My life will be over, but what can I do." The last was a statement, not a question.

"I believe that would be Officer Kathy Webb. And your life will not be over, Marti. It will not."

PROVERBS 24:25

"...those who rebuke the wicked will have delight..."

At two in the morning, the phone on Kathy's bedside stand jolted her out of sound sleep, waking J.D. as well. Forcing herself into alertness wasn't easy, but it helped to be out of bed and on her feet. She turned on a dim light beside the bed, and after asking questions of someone at the other end of the line, had said, "On my way," and hung up. J.D. was watching, concern on his face. He never asked questions and never failed to say, "Be careful out there." Kathy leaned across the bed and kissed him, then was throwing on a uniform; and zipping up warm outerwear, she had looked at J.D. and said, "Mitch found a body in the park. Driver's license says "Theodore Wencel Sweltzer" from "Des Moines." She knew he was remembering their recent conversation about Marti, too. She'd be making that phone call to Officer Osbourn in Des Moines after all. "Go back to sleep, Sweetie," and Kathy chuckled.

"Yeah! Right..." was the muffled response as J.D. pulled the blankets up around his neck and re-settled himself in his warm bed.

Kathy had gone to the park where the body was still on the bench. The wind had lessened considerably, and the snow was stopped but it had settled over the ice shell that had formed on the cooling body. Not knowing if it was a death due to natural causes or a homicide, yellow tape had been put around the area to be examined in the daylight. The pockets had been carefully searched for the wallet, which Kathy was now looking at by flashlight--at the same time, recalling the name of Martha Gracek Sweltzer as she read, "Theodore W. Sweltzer" on the driver's license. Pictures were taken, and the body was taken to the coroner.

Kathy had turned her back to the bench and her eyes searched the large old home across the street on the corner and her gaze rose to linger thoughtfully on the dim glow in the third level tower room. Mary-Marti must be awake. Reminding Mitch to put out the word to be on the lookout for the victim's car, both headed across the street towards the outside staircase on Fay Hessel's home. Kathy had no concern she would disturb the hard-of-hearing woman, and she had heard William was still staying in his nephew's home, but the other renter on the second floor would be alarmed at too much commotion.

The door at the top of the steps was unlocked, so Kathy entered, flashing her light down the hall and back, to the left where the steps leading to the top level were and began cautiously climbing the narrow steps to the door at the top which quite obviously was not latched. Filled with uneasy premonition, Kathy tapped on the door frame while calling out, "Police here!"

Mitch was a big man, and he filled the narrow staircase behind Kathy. Anyone who knew him didn't mess with him. He feared nothing. With the exception of tight places. Beads of sweat were starting on his forehead making him angry with himself. Mitch was claustrophobic. Kathy could hear him breathing behind her and pushed the door open wide and announced loudly again, "Police!" while entering the attic apartment.

Mitch followed, swinging his tactical torchlight swiftly into every shadowed corner. There was only silence. The officers moved apart, tense and alert. A single bulb gave out a dim light from the center of the attic. As Kathy aimed her flashlight into the alcove with Marti's bed, she heard Mitch call out he'd found a body. Turning towards his voice, she saw in the light of his torch a heap on the floor near an open doorway that looked to be a bathroom.

Kathy had a sick feeling as she thought of the sad, gentle woman she had met in the grocery store so recently. Mitch had stooped over the still form and was feeling for a pulse, but already shaking his head, "She's cold." Kathy did a double take when she knelt beside the body, and her voice held disbelief as well as confusion as she spoke. "This isn't Marti Gracek! What is going on here? I don't recognize this woman."

Mitch had leaned in for a closer look at the face of the dead woman. "Look at her eyes, Kathy. She's been strangled." The whites of the eyes had reddened, and petechiae was evident in the soft tissue around the eyes. In Kathy's opinion, Marti was ruled out as the killer. She did not believe such a small woman could succeed in strangling anyone, even someone as small as this victim.

In all the years of her police service, this one night would go down as the worst. And she had seen some bad things, too many times. A second crime scene was set up. Everyone available was called in. Time meant everything at this point. More pictures were taken; a close examination of surrounding areas was done. And as soon as possible, neighbors would be questioned.

The good citizens of Red wing woke to a new day and listened over morning coffee at their breakfast tables to radio and tv news of two separate murders, discovered as they slept soundly in their beds. In the midst of police hyperactivity, Kathy was notified a man was waiting to talk to her. She was about to send someone else to deal with him until the messenger relayed that the guy was looking for Marti Gracek. She had walked to the waiting room and looked closely at the tall man standing near the admissions desk, a dog sitting at his feet, its eyes fixed intently on its master.

As Kathy approached, the man noticed her and, guessing correctly, moved in her direction, the dog instantly following, which was when she saw the crippled leg of the animal. She did not make any request the dog be removed but raised an arm and pointed where she wanted them to talk privately and led the way back to her office. Un-noticed, the dog nosed to where Kathy had been standing, then it had picked up a faster gait, closing the distance to Kathy until it had its nose at her shoes and pant legs.

Chris had introduced himself as soon as Kathy had come out to him. Now they both stopped and watched as Gully continued his recognition of Marti's scent.

Kathy had become immobile believing she made a mistake in going soft on the devoted handicapped dog and wished she had banned the beast from the building. But Chris's reaction was one of joy, and he almost put his hands on the policewoman, but instead burst out with, "Gully knows you've been with Marti! Where is she—how is she?

"Come in here, Mr.---uh---Losinski." The tension had gone out of Kathy and she walked around her desk to sit down, with the dog following. "Why are you following Ms. Gracek, Mr. Losinski?"

"I believe she is running from her abusive husband, Ted Sweltzer. I wish she could have confided in me, but---she ran, six months ago. Left a note for me to look after Gully. He's Marti's dog," and Chris had waved a hand in Gully's direction where faint whines could be heard.

"Tell me, please. Is she okay? Where is she?" There was pleading in Chris's voice, and Kathy believed this man did care deeply for the missing Marti. Regretfully, she told him they had not located her yet, which did not necessarily mean something had happened to her. Chris told Kathy everything he had learned from Shirley, and in talking with Marti's family. He told Kathy what Marti's life had been, the three years in Decorah, before running again. When Kathy questioned him on his where-abouts since the day before, he was puzzled but answered truthfully; he had driven around the town on arriving, to determine where best to search.

Hearing Ted Sweltzer was found dead in the park during the night was obviously a shock to Chris, especially after having been questioned about his own activities and times in relation to Ted's demise. He had straightened in his chair and abruptly sat back in it; his eyes locked on Kathy's in disbelief. She had watched her words sink in for Chris, and he had slowly nodded his head, "Marti's safe, then. Finally," was all he'd said before adding, "She needs to know her mother is anxious to see her."

Kathy's estimation of Chris's good character rose still further but, regardless, she informed him not to leave town.

With the Losinski interview over, Kathy put the call through to Officer Osbourn in Des Moines. Ted had indeed been murdered, with one stab through the heart as cause of death, but so far, no weapon had been found. Deep, bloody scratches had been found on the backs of both hands of the dead man, as well as one scratch on the right wrist. With that information, Kathy expected to hear again soon that the dead woman in Marti's apartment had died at the hands of Ted Sweltzer.

The phone on Officer Osbourn's desk rang several times before he could get to it. It had been a hectic start for the day, and he expected nothing better was on the way. Some days just go that way. His "Hello" was abrupt. The female voice on the line identified herself, and where she was calling from bringing Tate to instant attention. He knew this would be something out of the ordinary. When Kathy informed Osbourn of having a murder victim from Des Moines under investigation, by the name of Theodore Sweltzer, Tate's butt hit the seat of his chair and he spoke unfiltered into the phone— "That son-of-a-bitch! We've been keeping an eye on him. Should have known he was on the move when his car hasn't left his father's driveway in almost a week!"

The conversation between Tate and Kathy answered many questions for both officers. Locating Martha-Mary-Marti was the biggest question left.

The Radstone residence was probably the only one in Minnesota that hadn't turned the news on at the breakfast table. Mornings were bad for Lucy, and Fern would carry breakfast to her on a tray after helping her up and assisting her in her personal care. Lucy's appetite had diminished drastically, and she did her best to eat dry toast and chicken broth. Her mornings exhausted her.

Marti had been in to help Fern in the care and had been close to weeping at the sight of the wasting body and terrible weakness of this kind and wonderful woman. The most shocking had been the still-visible scars where cigarettes had been put out on her back.

Lucy rested on her bed for a while and Marti went to the kitchen for toast and coffee, her own appetite gone. She knew as she poured a second cup of coffee, she was procrastinating on the phone call to the police station for Kathy Webb; and when she did make the call, she got a policeman who told her Officer Webb was unavailable at the moment. How could he help her? Marti gave him a phone number where Officer Webb could reach her and hung up.

Kathy was indeed unavailable. The coroner's report indicated the dead woman's airway had been crushed, and there were skin cells under her fingernails, believed to be from her struggle with her killer. No identification had been found on her, but a locked car had been parked a block away. Keys found in the victim's pocket had opened the car, and a purse found under the front seat held a driver's license belonging to the dead woman—a "Gaye Robertson." Calls to her residence went unanswered. There were more than a few Robertsons in the phonebook and Kathy was unprepared to call all of them, but the very first call--to someone unrelated to the woman, knew she was the wife of the owner of Del's Repair & Gas Station.

Asking to speak to Del, Kathy was put on hold briefly.

A cheerful male voice greeted her and asked what he could do for her. But when she asked if he was the husband of a Gaye Robertson, the cheerfulness left his voice. "Not anymore. We're divorced. Why do you ask?"

"We are investigating her death and will be talking to those closest to her. When could you come in, Mr. Robertson?" Kathy had heard the sharp intake of his breath and then a shocked, "What happened?"

"We are trying to find out, Mr. Robertson. How soon will you be here?"

"As soon as my mother can get here to look after my sons. Gaye didn't pick them up last night as planned."

Hardly had Kathy gotten off the phone with Del then she was handed the note with the phone number of some female who wanted to talk to her. The number had been traced to a "Lucy Radstone." Mitch had been to the house when he canvassed the neighborhood, but a housekeeper had answered the door saying Mrs. Radstone was "indisposed" or something like that, and that later in the day was better for her. For a brief span of time, the wheels went round and round in Kathy's head. Then she walked back out to her police car and drove to the Lucy Radstone address. She paused at the front door before ringing, looking from the drapes-covered front room window, down to the street and across into the park, past the park bench and across to where Martin's stand had been. Then she pushed the bell and waited.

When the door opened, an annoyed Fern snapped, "I told that last policeman Mrs. Radstone is not well. It will be noon at least, before she will be down."

Kathy knew ruffled feathers when she saw them, so she pleasantly and politely explained she believed someone else there had wanted to talk to her. Was that someone still there?

Fern was speechless with surprise, but before she could gather her wits, Kathy heard a soft voice from somewhere behind the fulsome form of the housekeeper say, "I called the policewoman, Fern. It's time I talked with her."

Fern turned to face the person behind her, and hadn't answered but gave a little nod, and briefly placed a hand on the thin shoulder of the small woman standing there. And Kathy finally had a look at the face that had been a mystery for months. No hat, no dark glasses; large, expressive eyes looked steadily back at her. Kathy stared, surprised by the completely white hair framing a delicate face, and thought, "Wow! She is beautiful."

Marti's head tilted slightly, and she looked past Kathy, behind her and a small frown of puzzlement appeared between the brows and her lips parted in confusion as she leaned a little forward. "What is all that?" and she pointed to all the yellow tape in the park. It looks like a...like a ...," Marti couldn't seem to finish the sentence.

"Like a crime scene?" Kathy finished. "Because that's what it is. There, and at your apartment."

The color drained from Marti's face, but she took a step closer to Kathy and looked to her left at Mrs. Hessel's property, but the shrubbery hid the yellow tape there. "What's happened? —Oh, dear God—what has he done?" And Marti fainted deadaway.

Kathy caught her before she could connect with floor, doorjamb, or cement stoop. If anything could have been more convincing of Marti's innocence of having anything to do with either murder, Kathy couldn't think of any.

When Marti regained consciousness and was able to get up, Kathy helped her into the living room and both women now sat facing each other on the two chairs in the window area. The drapes were still drawn, and Kathy left them closed out of consideration for the pale-faced woman in front of her, but she did turn the lamp on, and waited for Marti to begin. Whatever it had been that Ms. Gracek had wanted to discuss with the policewoman seemed to have been pushed to a back burner, so-to-speak, as Marti raised a hand in a feeble motion towards the park beyond the drapes and in a sick-sounding voice began, "What happened there?" Who---?" but couldn't finish the question.

Kathy felt pity for the woman in front of her. What was it about Martha Gracek Sweltzer that had sucked certain individuals into her orbit with such terrible outcomes for some?

"Your husband, Ted Sweltzer, was found on the bench there at two a.m. A homicide. Do you know a 'Gaye Robertson', Marti?"

The first part of Kathy's comment had caused a look of shock that morphed into one of confusion by the end of the statement.

"Not really. I know she's Del's ex-wife. I've never met her. Why?"

"She's the second homicide. In your apartment. Are you involved with Del Robertson"? That question appeared to offend Marti, and she answered with a slight chill in her voice.

"Involved? No. Friends? Yes. From over twenty years ago."

Kathy couldn't keep the surprise off her face as she asked, "Is he why you came here, Marti?"

The chilliness had gone from Marti's voice as she leaned back into the enveloping over-stuffed chair and, almost dreamily, told Kathy everything. It was a lengthy tale--hard to listen to at times, but Kathy listened, without interrupting, until the soft, almost unemotional voice became silent.

Kathy felt anger at--as well as let down by, the law enforcement she loved; that women should be afraid to go for help from those who were supposed to serve and protect. When help did come, it was often too late.

"You will need to remain in Red Wing for a while until we get a few things cleared up, Marti. You understand?" Marti nodded. "I also need to speak with Mrs. Radstone. Would she be available now?"

Marti responded that Fern would be the one to ask; and had then led the policewoman to the kitchen where Fern was mixing something in a large bowl on the wooden island. Cookies had cooled on a rack near the bowl and busy cook, but the kitchen still smelled of fresh baking.

Fern frowned and looked doubtful at Kathy's request to talk with Lucy but agreed to go upstairs and ask if she felt well enough to come down. Fern wasn't gone long but returned to say Lucy would see Officer Webb in her room if that was acceptable.

Marti offered to show the way to Lucy's room, and Fern returned to her work.

Kathy surreptitiously took note of Lucy's home as she passed through each room and admired the down-played elegance. Entering the sick woman's bedroom, not knowing what to expect, Kathy was surprised at the neatness of the well-lit attractive room done in soft pastels. Mrs. Radstone was nicely dressed, with every hair in place, and skillfully made up. But the prominence of bones, and the grayish skin tone couldn't be hidden. She didn't get up as Kathy approached but remained in the comfortable upholstered sitting room chair by a "lady's desk."

Lucy apologized for having kept Kathy waiting, explaining mornings were becoming more difficult for her recently, and then asked how she could be of help to the police. Marti pulled the desk chair out for Kathy, then looked at Lucy with great, sad eyes and left the room. Kathy proceeded to ask all the necessary questions of, "Had Lucy seen or heard anything unusual in the past twenty-four hours; did she have anything at all to add that would perhaps be useful to the police? Any suspicions of anything?"

And Lucy had nothing at all that she could contribute to help solve the tragic situation. When asked why Marti was obviously staying in Lucy's home while having her own apartment right next door, Lucy quietly explained with no self-pity in her voice that she was well aware she did not have much more time, and she preferred to spend it in her own home. Fern, a widow, took care of as much as she could, but was raising two of her own grandchildren and had to be at home each night for them, as well as some days. Having grown fond of Marti over the card games they frequently played, Lucy admitted she had talked her into calling in sick until it could be arranged for Marti to stay as long as she might be needed. Lucy could no longer be alone at night.

Pointing to a brass bell within her reach on the corner of her desk, and then in the direction of an adjoining bedroom, Lucy finished with, "Marti has that room so I'm not alone."

As seemingly open and pleasant as the interview had been, Kathy still left the sick woman's room with the niggling feeling she hadn't been told everything.

Kathy had been gifted with discernment but was also adept at reading body language. Her quiet attentiveness invited people to talk, often times to their own detriment. It was a mistake to underestimate her. Taking her time descending the stairs, she replayed the interview with Lucy, and could recall the odd pauses before answering some questions, the flicker of the eyelashes in the same way. The carefully worded answers. All well done, but with hints of rehearsal.

Marti met her at the base of the stairs to escort the policewoman out. As they neared the pocket doors to the living room, Kathy asked to have a look at something; and, though Marti was surprised, she agreed, nodding. After standing in the middle of the room, observing the two chairs in the window alcove, she moved forward to where she could pull the drapes open and looked out at the park. To the bench. Across the park to the houses facing the park from the other side. Kathy then sat down in one of the chairs and studied the scene laid out before her. Rising, she moved to the other chair, sat, and again studied the park. With a sigh, she let her hands fall to the cushion on each side of her thighs preparing to stand when something stopped her. Moving her fingers on her left between the cushion and the curved chair side, she tilted her head to look at what she was pulling into view. Binoculars. Turning and looking Marti in the eyes, Kathy asked her, "Did you know these were here?"

Surprise was Marti's reaction, but she admitted she knew Lucy was a bird watcher and had told her she used binoculars now that she couldn't get out to the park.

Kathy strongly suspected the woman upstairs wasn't telling everything.

Back at the police station Del waited for his interview with Officer Webb. A jumble of thoughts and emotions swirled in his mind. His phone at work had begun to ring off the hook right after Webb had delivered word of Gaye's murder. Murder! The word itself was unimaginable, and he couldn't believe it would happen to Gaye! How in hell had she gotten herself in a situation that this could happen? His mother had called him before he could call her to be with the boys. How—what—was he going to tell the boys? How would this affect them? He had rushed to get them out of school and back to their grandmother.

All he told them was, "Grandma will be with you till I get back. All I know, boys, is something has happened to your mother. It's bad. When I know more, we will sit down and talk. Okay? And he had left them, wide-eyed and anxious, in his mother's care and rushed back to the RWPD.

He was kept waiting, most of the time pacing. He wished they would hurry up and tell him what was going on. He wondered where he had been, what had he been doing while Gaye lost her life. Voting? Yesterday was election day, he'd been in a voting booth sometime in the morning, casting his vote for Jimmy Carter, running on his "Why Not the Best" motto. November 8th. Did it happen then? Or while he had lunch? He no longer had any feelings for her—she had been anything but the best! But dear God, he'd never wished her dead!

Sitting across from Del Robertson, Kathy's steady gaze missed nothing. The man appeared restless, agitated at times; and confused to learn his ex-wife was strangled in Marti's apartment. He returned to that fact twice, questioning why Gaye would be there. She didn't know Marti. She didn't know he had met Marti accidentally after a twenty-year span. He had been, and still was, interested in Marti; but Gaye didn't know that. There was no reason on God's green earth for her presence in Marti's apartment. When told of the threatening graffiti in the bathroom, Del had literally appeared to melt in his chair. All that Kathy observed told her this man had no involvement in Gaye's death, but Ted Sweltzer's death was something else altogether.

"What do you know about Ted Sweltzer, Mr. Robertson?" Kathy had sprung the change of subject on Del and watched his expression change. Surprised. Puzzled.

"Is that the guy found dead in the park? He killed Gaye?"

And then Del went silent, his thoughts had turned inward while seconds ticked past, and something had cleared up inside Del's head. "Ted. Marti mentioned her husband, Ted. The dead guy—he's her husband? Did he kill Gaye?"

"You've never met Ted Sweltzer? Did Marti tell you anything about him?"

"Never met him, no—but Marti did say the marriage had been abusive, and Ted didn't take her leaving well. I don't believe they were divorced. I do know she was afraid of him."

When Kathy asked him to verify where he was at the times of the two deaths, Del had stated he had been with his sons, waiting for Gaye to come for them.

Del felt stunned by all he had learned talking with Kathy, who watched as depression settled over the man in front of her.

"What will I tell my sons?" he had mumbled. Looking up at Kathy he stated, "God judges—that's not my job. Gaye was a difficult person to live with, but if she had made herself a problem to me after the divorce two years ago now—I would have filed a restraining order. My sons love their mother. I did not wish her dead. I need to get home to them, they are waiting for me, if you don't have any more questions."

Kathy didn't bother telling Del Robertson not to leave the area. She knew he wouldn't.

PROVERBS 29:25

"...but whoever trusts in the Lord is safe."

He had been walking around the outside of the park with Gully, avoiding the yellow tape. Chris and the dog had also passed by the yellow tape at the large house on the corner where he now knew Marti had rented. Had she already run again? Was there to be no catching up with her? Gully had caught her scent, but walked in circles, back and forth with low whines. Chris wondered how long he was expected to stay in town. Right now, it was a warm, sunny day with no sign of the snow from two days earlier, but it was November, and it was Minnesota so change could come swiftly. "Well, boy, since restaurants are out of the question, and you shouldn't be eating so many b-u-r-g-e-r-s, so let's go find a couple of sandwiches for each of us somewhere close and come back here to eat."

The plan hadn't been difficult or taken long. Chris pulled the car close to the park edge where there was a bench, and there man and dog sat down to share a meal as another figure neared them, "shambling" slowly. Chris knew what "homeless" looked like and he knew an army coat when he saw one. He slid over, leaving space for the shaggy man. The food sat in the middle of the bench and Chris spoke to the man who was now in front of him. "You're welcome, man. Enough here for you, me, and Gully."

The homeless man had quietly seated himself and picked up a sandwich. Holding it towards Chris, he mumbled, "T'anks," and Chris caught a quick glimpse of a chain at the edge of the loose collar under the open coat. Dog tags. Chris broke off chunks of sandwich for Gully to make his meal last a little longer.

The dog ate fast, then wanted Chris's, and their dinner companion watched silently--accepting more as it was offered, and Chris told the man about Gully. That Gulliver was named by Marti when he followed her home and never left. At the name of Marti, the rag-tag fellow had slowly reached out a hand and gently stroked the dog's nearest ear. Chris found himself holding his breath, relieved when Gully allowed the touch, then continued talking about the dog. "Gully knows his Marti has been here, but he just can't find her. Looking up, the man turned his head towards the houses across from the park before them, and raising an arm pointed and nodded. Chris looked at where the finger pointed and gave a disappointed sigh. "Yes, Marti lived there, but now she's gone again."

A rusty voice rasped, "No. Not there. There!" and the pointing finger made a small sweeping motion to the big house next door to Marti's rental.

Disbelief struggled with hope in Chris's heart, and he stood up to leave but first turned to the man on the bench and said,

"You're a good man, soldier. I thank you."

And slowly, Rolo stood up until his back was straight, his head was up, and looking Chris in the eye, gave a dignified nod.

Gully had also stood and was watching Chris's face. It was a poignant scene, quickly gone, but Kathy had seen it as she glided past in her police cruiser.

Standing on the front stoop of the Radstone home with a finger on the doorbell, Chris knew his pulse rate was racing. Now he pressed it and heard the chime faint and far away. Straining to listen for any sound indicating someone was coming, he wondered if Marti was indeed in this residence. About to press the bell a second time, he stopped. There came the sound of a heavy footfall and, disappointed, Chris knew it wasn't Marti's light footfall. The door was opened by a plump woman who wasn't particularly welcoming. She was wearing an apron and she had apparently dried her hands on it, so Chris felt fairly certain he had interrupted her in the kitchen. As he offered his apologies for bothering her, Gully had moved forward with his awkward gait, and the woman had stepped backwards in alarm, ready to close the door, but Gully was already across the threshold and heading down the hall, his head lifted, and his ears perked. The woman's voice was raised in anger, "Get that animal out of here or I'll call the police!"

Chris tried to defuse the situation, but finally all he could do was call to the dog, "Gully, come here, boy! Come on! Come here." But Gully was trying to navigate the curving stairs, ignoring Chris. He had heard what the other two had not— Marti's surprised "Gully!" from Lucy's bedroom. Now she was rushing from the room, through the hall to the stairs, and then she was flying down the stairs to the dog, still climbing awkwardly. Chris and Fern watched in fixed attention as Marti sat on a step and wrapped her arms around her dog and he licked her face while she murmured to him.

Chris had walked in and was at the base of the stairs unable to look away from finally seeing Marti again and knowing she was safe. He longed for her to trust him; he hoped that day would come soon. Now he waited for her to look at him.

Marti felt his presence and was afraid to face him. She hadn't trusted him enough to let him know how awful her life had been; and if she could have made such a bad choice with Ted, she didn't trust herself not to make the same mistake again. It had seemed a better choice to run, to depend upon herself. She never wanted to be trapped like that again.

Fern had slowly closed the front door and stepped a little closer to the stairs. Marti looked over Gully's head to Chris and knew he would make no demands on her or ask for an accounting from her. With Gully clinging close to her legs, she approached Chris but all she could do was fold her arms about her own rib cage and keep Chris outside the safe buffer zone. With tears falling, she thanked him with all her heart for his care for Gully. The change in the traumatized dog was impossible to miss.

A faint tinkle from a bell sounded from Lucy's room, and Marti asked Chris to wait for a minute while she enlightened Lucy about all the activity going on in her home. She had glanced at Gully as she started back and seeing him follow slowed her climb to accommodate him. The two of them disappeared down the hall, while Chris and Fern turned and looked at each other as Chris apologized for barging in, for disrupting her work, and she had kindly brushed it all away, saying she should have realized who he was. Marti had talked of him recently, and of her dog. She should have known. Then quickly she briefed him that Ms. Lucy was quite ill upstairs, but she would no doubt be pleased to see him if she was up to it.

Moments later, Marti leaned over the bannister and signaled for Chris to come upstairs.

Giving Fern a grateful smile and nod, he joined Marti

waiting at an open door.

Turning, she led him into the restful pastel bedroom, and to a fragile-looking woman seated in an upholstered chair that matched the drapes and bedspread.

Chris was quick picking up on things. And he knew the woman looking into his soul with her piercing blue eyes was dying. On her own terms. In all her frailty and physical weakness, Chris recognized a strong woman. He had gently taken the cold bony hand, enveloping it in his large hand, warming hers. Marti placed the desk chair by him to sit; and Chris discovered Lucy was interested in anything and everything he had to say. They openly talked of the tragedy in Marti's apartment, and of Ted's murder in the park. They spoke with certainty that Gaye had tragically died at Ted's hands, but what happened to Ted, no one had offered up so much as a guess. That was a mystery.

Fern bustled in carrying a tray with cups and cookies, then went back for the coffee. It was a welcome and refreshing break, especially for Lucy.

Chris was aware of the way both Fern and Marti watched over Lucy, and he knew not to make his stay too long. A load had been lifted from him knowing Marti was alive and well— he looked forward to the next phone call to Nancy Bolin. With that thought, Chris turned to Marti and asked if she had spoken with her mother yet and he had his answer before she spoke when her face lit in a smile of joy: "Oh, yes! It was wonderful! They are coming to see me, Mom and Julia, and Harold—I've never met him!" Her happiness was wonderful to see, and he thought, "It took Ted dying for Marti to live again. What made some people so evil that their death made the world a better place?"

Then looking back to Lucy a short while later, Chris thanked her for seeing him, that he was grateful for the visit, but would be on his way now. Turning, he'd looked questioningly at Marti and she had risen, telling Lucy she would see

Chris out. Gully followed his two people out the bedroom door, making his slow and cautious way down the steps under their watchful eyes.

At the door, for a long moment, they had looked at each other in silence, Marti with troubled eyes. In a quiet voice, Chris told her, "You know where you can find me, Marti. Any time." After a few seconds pause, he looked down at Gully and said, "I'll look after him until you get settled again. I think stairs are getting too hard for him." Calling the dog, they stepped outside the door--and Marti began closing it, then impulsively stepped forward and hugged Chris fiercely, her head on his shoulder, then quickly stepped back and closed the door. Chris's face lit with hope, and his step was lighter.

On the other side of the door, Marti was standing, head hanging low, shoulders drooping, a feeling of depression heavy on her. Then she retraced her way back to Lucy's room, knowing her friend had used what little strength she had to meet Chris--learn something about him; but Marti knew she and Fern would be helping Lucy into bed earlier tonight. There would be no card game. She didn't want to think about what was coming.

Lucy's eyes were closed when Marti returned, but they opened as she approached her.

"Do you need to lie down, Lucy?" Marti asked as she reached for the bell to summon Fern to help."

"Yes, that sounds good—just a lie-down for a short bit. I'll lie on the bed cover—a throw will be all I need."

Marti leaned over the bed, placing the pillow on top of the bed cover after ringing the hand bell for Fern, who responded quickly. The two of them helped the weak woman onto her bed, covering her with a soft warm throw.

"I'll call when I am ready to be up. Just leave the bell in reach," and Lucy's sweet smile was her thanks to them.

Marti restored order in the room as Fern gently smoothed the throw over Lucy's feet, and returned to the kitchen. As

Marti finished and was about to follow Fern, Lucy held a trembling hand out to her and Marti had immediately reached for it with both hands, trying to warm the coldness away, and found herself sitting on the edge of the soft bed.

"Marti, Marti. My dear Marti," was a whisper. "Don't let fear rule. The price will be your happiness." Lucy's eyes closed.

As her hand relaxed in Marti's hands, Marti slowly placed the cold hand under the throw, then rose and left without a sound.

In the kitchen, Fern was putting together a menu to appeal to the sick woman as well as nourish her. Marti began washing up the used utensils and putting the kitchen in order. Fern's eyes were red-rimmed, and she didn't feel like talking. Marti knew how hard Fern's life was, a hand-to-mouth existence with no savings. The two grandchildren were dependent on their grandmother, since their mother had died, and the father had simply walked away.

But Marti also knew something Fern didn't. When Lucy had gotten the card-playing started between them, Marti had arrived for a usual game and found a well-dressed man in his sixties, seated in the living room with Lucy: her lawyer. She had asked Marti to be a witness to her will. A will leaving everything to Fern. She had been sworn to secrecy. Fern was going to be just fine.

The yellow tape had been removed. Kathy had re-interviewed all the parties connected to Ted's death. With no evidence against anyone, no arrests had been made. She hadn't talked to Rolo in any depth. The man seemed unstable, but she had seen Chris carrying on what looked like a normal exchange and she wondered if Rolo may have seen something. But Kathy needed another visit with the terminally ill woman. She didn't want to, but maybe one more non-pressure talk wouldn't hurt. So, Kathy casually drove by the park, randomly, for several days before seeing Rolo walking out from among the evergreens. She had chocolate bars in a pocket as she left her cruiser at the park curb and approached Rolo who pretended not to see her. "Hi, Rolo. Everything going okay? It's been quite a mess here recently, right?"

The man's response had been a combination of head shakes and mumblings.

"Did you happen to see anything that happened to the man found dead on that bench?" and Kathy had pointed at the bench in question, not far from them.

What Kathy clearly heard was, "Bad man. Bad man!" and Rolo reacted in agitation and shook his hands as if shaking off dirt. Any further effort to converse only agitated the man more and Kathy left him to himself after offering him the chocolate bars.

He watched intently as Kathy left, heading through the park and across the street to climb the steps of the sloping yard. And, as before, Fern answered the door, obviously not happy to see the policewoman on the front step.

"Officer Webb. If you are here to see Mrs. Radstone, her health has not improved, and she really is in no condition to be upset."

"I appreciate what you are saying, and I agree. Mrs. Radstone should not be made upset. I assure you, that is not my intention. I do need to speak with her one more time. I ask for ten minutes—less if I feel that to be best."

Fern stood silently, weighing what was best to do, then grudgingly stepped to the side, disapproval showing on the good woman's face.

Kathy gave a gracious, "Thank you," followed by, "I remember the way." Then disappearing up the winding stairs and balcony. Giving a light tap-tap on the doorjamb, Kathy entered the sickroom. Partially drawn drapes filtered the weak sunlight, leaving the quiet room in a somber dimness. Marti sat in a chair at the bedside, an open book on her lap.

Lucy was awake, a long thin form barely mounding the bed coverings. The voice was weaker, but clear. "How nice to see you, Officer Webb. Come closer, please. Marti reads my favorite books to me—she is, no doubt, ready for a break."

Marti had placed the book on the night table and touched Lucy's hand, promising to be back when the policewoman's business was finished and she had soundlessly left after nodding a greeting to Kathy, with a small smile.

Kathy sat down where Marti had been, and leaned near to Lucy, and in a soft, unaccusing, almost amused voice, looked into the intelligent blue eyes and said, "You haven't fooled me, Lucy. I know you know who killed Ted Sweltzer." It was all said so deliberately, but patiently.

Lucy looked back as though a joke had been shared and smiled. But said nothing.

Still Kathy looked into the crystal blue eyes. "Tell me," she said.

But again, no answer.

A great sadness came over Lucy's face, and finally the weak voice, "Some people aren't fit to live—should never have been born."

"One more question, Lucy," Kathy's voice had a pleading note in it, close to a whisper, too. "Do you know why he was killed here?"

Lucy had nodded as tears slipped down the sides of her face.

"Will you tell me?"

But Lucy's mouth formed a whispery, "No."

Kathy's strong, warm hand had gently covered the bony hand lying at Lucy's side, lingering. Then she thanked Lucy for seeing her, and left without meeting Fern, but Marti was waiting in the entry.

Kathy felt depressed. "I really am sorry; it was necessary. But I hope I haven't made it worse for her."

Almost as if she were thinking out loud, Marti spoke, "I

asked Lucy who could do such a thing, and she said, "Someone with nothing to lose."

Kathy felt riveted to the floor and her mind went into overdrive. As the door closed with a click behind her, Kathy knew she would not be pressing Lucy for any further details on the Sweltzer case. But now she was laser-focused on two—yes, two suspect persons!

Looking over the reports of interviews with people living near the park, Kathy focused most on Martin. Mitch had filled out that report with the fact Martin was sick; had answered the door in robe and slippers mid-day, unshaven, coughing, and had stated he had the flu all week. Mitch confirmed he believed Martin.

Rolo was a different matter. Kathy viewed him more and more as knowing, seeing, and hearing more than he revealed. There was something foxlike about him. She had witnessed him appearing from sheltering trees and bushes. Getting him to communicate was a waste of time, but she felt sure he knew more than anyone could guess. That Lucy knew and wouldn't tell indicated it was a local-- a neighbor she knew well and trusted? That was no danger to anyone else?

Word had reached Kathy's ears of Ted's unprovoked attack on Rolo on the park bench, and she recalled his furious, "Bad man, bad man" statement. Gossip had it that he had been a soldier, so killing a "bad man" might have seemed the thing to do.

Lucy was slipping away a little more every day and both Fern and Marti knew the end was near. The doctor came daily, and Lucy was kept comfortable, but no longer spoke. Fern stayed as much as she could, but Marti had given notice to the nursing home and spent all her time at Lucy's side. She had also removed her few personal belongings from Fay's attic and had struggled through an ear-splitting conversation with the hard-of-hearing landlady as she terminated her rental obligations. Fay was sorry to have Marti leave, and in her usual unfiltered way wished Marti well and hoped her bad luck had ended.

Marti had time to think about her future as she looked after Lucy. It had been wonderful seeing her family again; and Harold had truly been a delightful man. She was happy for her mother. Julia looked wonderful, and was happily single, with work she loved. It would be so good for Marti to be with her family again after so many lost years. Marti had kept up on Gully with phone calls to Chris; and had enjoyed talks with Shirley as well as Thora. She was happy for the first time since she married Ted and grateful to not be looking over her shoulder for him. She felt free.

Kathy had been looking forward to a post-Thanksgiving weekend, planning on a return visit with Martin on Monday, but woke up Sunday morning aching all over with a vicious headache; and then the stomach went. Kathy came down with a nasty flu and was sick the entire following week. When she felt well enough to return to work, it was to find a request for a wellness check at a residence where the postman reported piled up mail and newspapers. The home belonged to Martin, and Kathy felt the growing apprehension the closer she was to the address.

Mitch forced the kitchen door lock as it was easiest. A neighbor stood at his yard's edge and called out that he hadn't seen any lights on in several days. The kitchen looked uncared for, cluttered with unwashed dishes. The stove was gas, but there was no odor of gas. Kathy and Mitch walked through each silent and uncared for room on the ground floor. There had been no response to their calling Martin's name, and they made their way through the upstairs with no evidence of the homeowner other than scattered clothing and an unmade bed.

"Does he have family he would have gone to stay with?" Mitch asked.

Kathy had to say she didn't know.

And Mitch had answered in one word, "Garage," and they retraced their way back to the ground floor and from there into the garage where Martin's car was still in its parking space. As Mitch reached the driver's side, he abruptly stopped and, to Kathy's surprise, he swore! Stepping around him she saw Martin slumped forward over the steering wheel—and she retched. Her stomach was not back to normal, and to see the good-natured, kind man dead by his own hand sickened her. Time and carbon monoxide had destroyed any resemblance of the man she had known. If she hadn't gotten sick—if she hadn't missed checking with him that Monday...if...if...!

He had fastened a hose from the tail pipe into the car window. The key was in the "On" position. The gas had run out but not before doing what Martin intended.

Yellow tape was again in evidence, on the opposite side of the park this time, and a search was in progress for a note or letter. None was found. But no evidence was found that it was other than suicide. And the neighbor who reported no lights for several days had later emotionally related how the arson of Martin's dead son's food stand had absolutely crushed Martin. It was all he had left of his only child.

"Someone who had nothing to lose," echoed in Kathy's head, as pieces of information fit together like pieces in a puzzle.

She had gone back out through the kitchen and stood on the walk facing the park, her eyes going from the empty space where the unique hand-crafted stand had been for years, across the park to the bench where Ted died, then further to Lucy's front room windows which had a birds-eye view of everything. As she stood there letting everything fall naturally into place, Rolo had made his slow shuffling way to the area of ground in front of the burned area and there he stopped, looking across the street at Kathy before looking at the ground at his feet. In a few moments, he looked again at Kathy, and pointed at a spot near where he stood, and she had crossed over at record speed. But for as hard as she studied the ground nothing unusual was observable, and frustrated, she looked back at Rolo, who clenched a fist as though holding a knife, and then made an upward thrust. "Bad man!" he muttered and pointed a finger at the ground again and mimed shoving a blade into the ground.

Ah! She got his meaning, and dropped to a knee, scraping away at dead grass and dirt. Mitch had joined them and pulled out his jack knife to begin digging at the area Rolo was pointing to. A metallic click was heard and in short order, a dirt-covered knife was slowly pried out of the ground.

"Rolo—I owe you—big time." Kathy knew she would be bringing hot sandwiches to Rolo throughout the cold winter that was on its way. But for now, she needed to ask the hard questions. "Did you see when this was put in the ground?"

Rolo nodded.

"Did you see the bad man die?"

This time, Rolo answered with a clear, "Yes."

Both Kathy and Mitch thanked Rolo, in unison, and headed back into Martin's sad, abandoned home to the kitchen and together rummaged through all the knife and utensil drawers until a set of matching knives was found, photographed, bagged, tagged, etc. Martin, it appeared, was Ted's killer.

Ted's body had been returned to Des Moines for burial. His sisters had dealt with what was necessary and proper, but there was no visitation, or funeral service. Peggy had asked Donna if she could remember the location in the Bible of the brutal king who ruled for a few years, then died and no one missed him? Donna recalled the scripture, but not the location, then added, "Maybe we should have had a funeral service with those verses," and Peggy responded, "Not missing Ted is a given. Forgetting him would be preferable." They sent all the bills to their father and left their family home for the last time.

Kathy sent photographs of all of Ted's jewelry and wallet contents to the DMPD addressed to Officer Osbourn along with a full report of the case. Fully engrossed with the photos, and using a magnifier, Osbourn had been revisiting the cold case of Audra O'Neil, verifying in the records that the victim was missing a ruby-diamond ring she never took off; said to be the last gift her father had given her. The father and daughter had a close bond. With the aid of the magnifying glass, he knew he was looking at a ring that matched the description of the one the victim's friends all testified to as being missing. Taking a deep breath, he straightened and reached for a notepad, wrote a name and address down, then picked up his phone and summoned Joe to run an errand for him. Joe was by nature a happy-go-lucky man, known for his good humor and practical jokes. He had been happily engaged in flirting with an attractive young female officer when Tate interrupted, wanting him in his office. Tate noted Joe's usual jaunty smile had vanished.

"Having a bad day, Joe?"

"Actually, it *was* going quite nicely."

"Did I interrupt something important, Joe?"

"Ahhhh—no-o—," the good nature was back. "What do you want?"

Joe had reached Osbourn's desk and leaned over the papers with interest.

"Information came in on a cold case. Audra O'Neil? The missing ring?"

Joe had frowned, scratching a cheek bone, concentrating.

"New Year's Eve. Fall from a balcony, right?"

"You got it. Here's a photo of it."

And Osbourn filled Joe in with the details and told him to follow it up with a visit to O'Neil's best friend, Patrice Holman; see if she IDs it.

Studying the address, Joe was on his way. Joe was happy with his assignment. He was glad to be out of the office, mixing with the Christmas crowds. The traffic was heavy which never bothered him, as he approached it not only as a challenge, but an opportunity to practice his driving skills. His speedy reflexes and driving skills were legendary, but none of his relatives got in any car with Joe behind the wheel. He wasn't surprised to learn Patrice Holman was not at home—he had already figured she'd be out and about, but not wanting to go back to the office, he decided to follow her to her hairdresser.

He wasn't made welcome at the posh establishment, but Joe wasn't one to be bothered by hoity-toity. Truthfully, he enjoyed offending them. He left behind an irritated best friend of Audra O'Neil, but she had taken one look at the photo of the ring, grabbing it, and excitedly saying, "That's it! That's Audra's ring!" Then she had turned snappy again demanding to know why they had been so slow in finding it!

Joe took his time going back to headquarters, driving through downtown admiring all the Christmas decorations, wishing he could have had a closer look at the Younker's store windows. He knew Tate would be happy with the report, so he had no shame in exaggerating why it took so long to do such an easy assignment. When asked what took so long, Joe wove a long tale of awful traffic; having to locate the woman—whatever; of how uncooperative she was, until Tate told him to shut up and just get to the report.

The cold case was re-opened, and a court order allowed a search of all of Ted Sweltzer's residence which turned up a New Year's costume in a storage rental that matched a picture of a man exiting the hotel close to five a.m.

MARTI

Christmas was evident on the streets of Red Wing and in all the store windows; lighted trees could be seen in windows of homes as darkness came on early in the evenings. In Lucy's home no sign of Christmas was seen. Drapes were closed by four-thirty p.m., and inside was a heavy quietness, a time of waiting for the cancer to finish its course. Lucy would not see Christmas. The doctor had been called and Fern and Marti stood at the bedside watching as he listened for the beat of a heart, already knowing Lucy's suffering was over.

It was necessary for Marti to stay a little longer at the request of Lucy's lawyer, but her plans were to leave Red Wing. Ted had brought so much destruction to this town which had a special place in her memory that she no longer wanted to be there. For a while, at least, she wanted to be close to her family. She had told Chris of her plans during her last phone call and he had insisted he be the one to drive her and Gully to her family when she was ready to go. Del had come by with his sons to say good-bye and wish her well. He had looked at her with sadness and regret. She knew he had harbored hope for a future with the two of them; now he looped an arm over each boy and, turning, walked away. He didn't look back.

Fern and Marti had gone together to the lawyer's office for the reading of the will. Watching Fern's shock and amazement at Lucy's goodness to her brought joy to Marti as well. Fern and her grandchildren would be fine now. Lucy left her considerable jewelry to Marti to do with as she wished. Marti had hoped to say good-bye to Rolo but, as the cold had settled in, he appeared less frequently, and days had passed with no sign of him. Fern told her that was his usual pattern. She didn't know where he went or where he stayed. He didn't like to be bothered.

Marti's last good-byes had been made. It had been a brief stay in Red Wing, but she had formed attachments to several of its residents that she regretted leaving behind. Fay's devoted grandson, Gordon, had always been a friendly and outgoing young man—so willing to be helpful to her. Fay, too, she had liked very much despite the difficult communication with her. The occasional letter would be an easy way to keep in touch with Fay who craved human interaction.

Fern was hard to part from, but Marti knew she would make the effort to see her again. It had been an emotional good-bye.

Even Mincemeat, who had moved himself indoors, had seen Marti to the door. But being a self-loving creature—making sure he was on the warm side of door when it closed, he drew the line at stepping out on the frigid stoop with Fern when she gave a last hug to Marti. Looking in at the beat-up old fellow, she wondered if he would still be around in another year.

Chris and Gully waited for Marti in the car. Her bicycle lay in the open car trunk—Marti had one more stop before leaving for her mother's home. Waving to Fern on the stoop, Chris headed for downtown to the police station for the last stop.

Gully exited the car with his people, and Chris lifted the bicycle from the trunk and closed the lid while Marti entered the building in search of Kathy. Marti had called ahead and was expected. Kathy had risen from behind her desk and come around holding out a hand to Marti and giving her a big smile.

Marti spoke first, "I want to thank you for all you've done for me. Especially, just hearing me out and believing in me. I hope I see you again someday. Chris has taken my bike out to your parking area. I hope you might know some young girl who could use it." Marti said her "good-bye," letting Kathy know she would be at her mother's home in Rochester for now.

The ride to the Bolin residence in Rochester was mostly quiet but Chris had gently quizzed Marti about her plans for the future, which made her uneasy. All she knew for sure was she wanted time to re-connect with her family. She was not worried about her future, that much she knew. She had confidence in herself to find work to sustain herself. She had a CNA certificate; and if she preferred housekeeping, she knew she did excellent work. She was in an okay spot, and she was grateful.

Chris delivered Marti into the arms of her welcoming family for a long-overdue reunion. It was hard to hand over Gully, and say his good-byes, but knowing a healing time was beginning for Marti, he could only be happy for her. And finally, he was at peace knowing she was safe and could enjoy her life once more.

For Chris, it was a lonely drive back to Decorah. He returned to his old routine in his home, now that Gully was gone, leaving his workplace with a sense of abandonment. He put the food and water bowls out of sight along with the dog's bedding. When he'd put in his working hours, he was glad to leave.

Gilbert and Thora also felt lost without Marti inhabiting their "barn," for visits and occasional meals to share. The quiet seemed overwhelming, at times.

Marti bared her soul one final time, a purge essentially, to her mother and sister ending with, "It's done. Over. I will never speak his name again." No one ever mentioned him again.

The time between daughter and mother was cathartic for Marti. Julia came often, renewing their sister bonds. The old Marti began emerging. No longer shrinking; or lowering her head. The invisible persona began to vanish as much as the boniness. She blossomed again, laughed out loud without fear.

And then she had Harold teach her to once again be comfortable behind the steering wheel of a car. He drove her to the licensing bureau where she passed her test for a driver's license.

It was a leap, then, to deciding to sell Lucy's jewelry—except for one special piece—and buying her own car. She laughed with Julia over feeling like a teenager again with owning her very own first car.

Julia had grabbed Marti in a hard hug as she resisted crying over her sister's lost years. And she worried that Marti might fall into the pattern of the grown child who never leaves home. But she kept her thoughts to herself and spent as much time as she could with her sister.

With the return of a blooming spring, Marti broached her sister with a wish to visit her friend, Shirley, in Des Moines. She never mentioned needing to conquer feelings about her life there, but she knew she wouldn't feel completely free until she faced the city where so much of her life had been wasted.

Julia was disturbed at the thought, but as she watched Marti's "come-back," she reached the conclusion if that was what Marti felt she needed to do, then that was what they would do, and have a great time while they were at it!

Marti phoned Shirley and casually mentioned a wish for a weekend visit which was received joyfully by Marti's loyal friend and it was quickly a "done deal." Marti and Julia would soon be on their way in Marti's almost-new car to Des Moines.

The visit to the Hebners was a celebratory event, and the couple welcomed Julia, too, like an old friend. Shirley was crying tears of joy on seeing the healthy, happy Marti. Ted was not discussed but Shirley mentioned a hope that Marti would visit the police officer, Tate Osbourn, relating how he had tried to help Marti, how the man knew she had not felt safe with the police and that had bothered him very much.

Leaving the Hebners and pulling out into the traffic, the sisters had been quiet, both thinking over the pleasant hours spent in the company of the wonderful couple. Shirley had been a "safe harbor" for Marti at a critical time of her life and Marti was mulling over the things relayed to her about Officer Osbourn. She remembered him clearly as well as how close she had come to turning to him for help at that terrible time. She heard herself asking Julia, "Do you mind if I make one more stop?"

"Sweetie, whatever you want, I'm fine with," giving her sister a companionable pat on the shoulder.

"It will be a quick stop, won't take long," and a short while later they were stopped at a parking meter close to the police station and Julia was looking questioningly at Marti. Once in the waiting area and looking around, Marti wished she had not made this choice as memories of the abduction attempt rushed back. She had not expected that. Clenching her teeth, her resolve to never run from anything ever again returned a little at a time. A female officer at a window was watching, and gave her an encouraging look, asking if she needed help and

Marti had stepped up to the officer behind the counter, "I really don't need anything, but I did want to stop in before leaving town to say 'hello' to Officer Osbourn. I'm Marti Gracek and I wanted to let him know I'm doing well."

If you'd have a seat, I'll let him know you're here," and she had picked up the phone and could be seen speaking to someone on the other end, followed by a short pause and she hung up, flashing a smile in their direction and returned to the papers on her desk.

In moments, Osbourn was striding into the waiting area, a delighted smile on his face as he scanned the room for her. It took a second look, as she rose and moved towards him, for him to recognize her and his face lit with pleasure as he told her she did indeed look fine as he reached out both hands to shake her hand.

Her instinct years earlier was right on the mark: Tate Osbourn was a man of good character and she should have trusted him. They conversed as old friends might have done, surprising Marti.

When she remembered Julia's presence, she had turned to her sister and made the introduction, and Tate had again stepped forward with a hand extended, greeting Julia warmly, remarking on the sisters' similarity. And Julia was mute, starry-eyed, not at all her usual confident, out-going self. The happily single Julia fell in love-at-first sight! And Tate was not unaware of the chemistry. He had their phone numbers by the time the visit was over, and Marti led her sister back to the car where she laughed till she had to wipe her eyes.

It came as no surprise then, when a few weeks later, Julia informed everyone she was transferring to Des Moines to work--and in short order had done so. Marti missed the frequent visits with Julia but was too happy for her to want it otherwise.

She had been consumed with wanting to catch up for all she had missed out on with her mother, but Marti had begun feeling restless recently. The decision to leave the Bolin residence had come suddenly and easily one evening as she was stirring stroganoff sauce at the stove and in glancing at her mother as Nancy passed her husband in his chair, watching the news, she had bent and kissed the bald spot on the top of his head and touched his cheek with the tips of her fingers.

"I don't want to live my life alone," rang like a bell in Marti's heart as she observed the contentment of her mother and stepfather. That night, looking around her mother's guest room—now Marti's room—she knew she was ready to go back to Decorah. Gully would like that, too. He went with her everywhere, but she could see he was aging. His muzzle was white; and stairs were so hard for him. She had begun lifting him in and out of the car. And she knew he missed Chris. "So do I," she thought. Decorah seemed like "home" to her. She had been happy there, had started to feel like she belonged there. Until---the night "*he*" found her. But that was over now, she knew that. He had finally hurt the wrong person and in the process set her free. It was time she and Gully went home.

Breakfast with her mother and Harold was over, and seconds on coffee had been poured when Marti told them of her plan to move on. Back to Decorah and Chris. It was a charming town and she had friends there. Besides, it was home to Gulliver, and it was time to be moving on. She could see the anxiety on her mother's face, though she accepted what Marti told her, but she was emphatic in making sure her daughter knew she was always welcome at their home, too. Harold had nodded while reaching for Nancy's hand.

That night, Marti deliberated on calling Chris first before leaving, then vacillated. "Call? or show up?" and finally decided to show up. She would know by his face what his feelings were when he saw her. Decorah was where she wanted to be. With, or without, Chris. And Gully deserved to go home.

Readying for the trip was simple; all she had was a dog, a suitcase, and a car. Her mother had put on a brave face, determined to be happy for her daughter but in the rearview mirror Marti saw her mother with Harold's arms around her, crying on his shoulder. Marti cried tears of empathy for quite a few miles. The natural scenery spread out on both sides of the highway from Minnesota into Iowa was beautiful and being able to drive herself in a car of her own was so liberating. It was an uneventful trip, with one stop at a McDonald's for Gully's favorite chow. And she shared her ice cream shake with a very happy dog.

Chris had immersed himself in his work again. His customers were happy, and he slept well at night, but day followed day in a frighteningly monotonous way. He had finished a tall chiffonier for a client who was due to arrive soon. It was an impressive reproduction of an antique original the family had lost in a fire. Chris headed to his office to fill out the paperwork and enter everything into his meticulous records. He wondered how long it had been since Marti called. Maybe this evening a call would come. Or maybe he should call her. The doorbell jingled and he startled. The guy must be early to pick up his "prize" and Chris called out he'd be with him in a minute, then continued finishing his records. An odd, uneven clicking sound was coming closer to his office and puzzled, he stood up behind his desk, his eyes on the door, a frown forming between his brows. About to call out again, Gully in his awkward gait was heading for Chris as fast as he could, the nails on his front leg clicking on the wood floor.

"Ahhhh, Gully! Come here, boy; Lord, I've missed you!" and kneeling on one knee, Chris hugged the dog. When he looked up, Marti was standing in the doorway watching him, silent as always and he couldn't look away from the transformation. The boniness had disappeared, replaced by healthy curves. Her face had a softness, she was even younger looking.

"Are you back to stay?" He had to know.

"Yes. I thought Gully should come home again."

It was harder to ask the next question but after a pause

it was out— "Am I in the picture?" and he held his breath, waiting.

"I'm hoping so, Chris."

He was still kneeling, and his smile was increasing, crinkles appeared at the corners of his eyes, and he opened his mouth to speak—and Marti knew what was coming—when the bell over the shop door jingled and voices could be heard exclaiming over the finished-- and other half-finished work-in-progress--in the show area. Chris gritted his teeth and Marti smothered a laugh.

"Be right there," he called. Then stood and swiftly wrapped Marti in a passionate embrace for all of two seconds, then stepped reluctantly around her, and went to deal with the customers. The client had brought his wife along this time as well two hefty-looking teenagers--their sons, to tackle the transport of the cumbersome piece.

Marti, with the ever-watchful Gully by her side, came to observe the exuberant family as they expressed their approval of the keepsake furniture Chris had created for them. The happy hubbub went out the door with the satisfied customers, leaving Chris and Marti facing each other with so much to talk over, plans to put in place, hope for their future together.

Following Marti outside, Chris admired her car and had then raised Marti's arm over her head with her driver's license clutched in her hand and declared her *the winner!* And they both laughed--and held each other before making their way to Thora and Gilbert's kitchen door.

Thora had bustled to open the door, bewildered by the "rat-a-tat-a-tat" knock, and on seeing Marti had literally screamed, throwing her arms in the air as she rushed at her, hugging her joyfully.

Gilbert, who had been restfully watching tv in his recliner had heard Thora's scream and floundered wildly trying to get up. When he heard her calls to "Come quickly, come see who's here," he was almost to the kitchen and was so glad to see Marti he never mentioned Thora's scream almost gave him a heart attack.

Marti felt close to tears at the welcome the elderly couple showered on her.

They had gathered around Thora's kitchen table with the smell of sugar cookies still lingering in the air from the baking she had done for a meeting at church the next day. They knew from Chris all that had happened in Red Wing and nothing was brought up to spoil their reunion.

Thora insisted Marti stay with them until she and Chris had everything figured out between them. And Gully was welcome as well.

Stuff, "things" were immaterial to Marti. She was restless, unsettled. Chris wanted Marti to choose where they would live once they were married, but she was unable to make a decision. He had observed her standing in the Iversons' yard looking up at the apartment over the barn--and watching Gully.

They had set a wedding date for a small, simple ceremony in the chapel of the church Chris attended. Marti's family and the Iversons were the only witnesses. Two weeks before the wedding, Marti had talked with Chris about needing to face all her fears in order to overcome them. She wanted to return to her apartment which she had fled in terror. It had been hers. It had been a place where she felt safe and happy. She wanted it back. But Gully couldn't do the steps. Chris had listened and agreed with her.

The Iversons certainly wanted them there. And workwise, it couldn't be better. It would be a tight fit, but he agreed to less is better, smaller is less to care for. As for Gully, Chris could easily install a small lift for the "old guy"—he was sure the Iversons would be okay with that.

With their approval, Chris began work on Marti's, Gully's, and his simple apartment.

The wedding ceremony had been simple but memorable,

as well as happy, and followed by an elegant surf-and-turf dinner at a great restaurant. Julia and Tate were witnesses on the marriage certificate. Julia was wearing a beautiful diamond and another wedding was not far off.

SIX MONTHS LATER

Marti and Gully were busy at Chris's desk balancing the books, paying the bills, and pausing to listen to the sounds from the work area. Chris was a whistler, a good one, and he favored all the good old hymns in particular as he worked his magic on the fragrant wood. Gilbert often wandered in and out, entranced as he watched Chris's hands craft works of art from plain boards. He had wondered for a while why he had failed at what Chris did with such ease. But when he'd thought more about that, he knew *he* was particularly good with his violin, which was a mystery to Chris. Guess everyone was given something special if they could figure out what it was and get serious. Which made him think of Marti. She was taking violin lessons from him again. And she did have talent.

Hearing Gilbert in the workroom talking to Chris, Marti left the paperwork for a few minutes' break and joined the men. Gilbert was still amazed whenever he looked at Marti to see such a physical change in her. Her walk was freer, her head was up, eyes wide and direct, no dark glasses. And so healthy-looking. No fading wallflower, as it were. But Thora and Gilbert, as well as Chris, knew that inwardly Marti was troubled. Each knew there was no way anyone could know exactly what she had been put through for so many years. Without a doubt a mark had been left. Marti took solitary walks, with Gully trailing, when the quiet times came. They gave her the space she needed, making sure she knew they were there for her.

A smile was instantly on her face as she spotted the covered tin in Gilbert's hands.

"Okay! What did Thora make this time, Gil? Let's see!" and he had laughed, demanding to know if she had hot coffee in the office to go with the surprise. He knew Chris and Marti well. They always had a large coffee maker plugged in, with disposable cups handy. He placed the tin on the neat desk and pried the lid off as the couple poured the coffee. Marti asked if Thora was on her way over and was informed, she had been picked up by a member of her women's group and would be out for the afternoon. He claimed he "stole" the tin of treats, but it was obvious Thora had prepared the "rosettes" especially for a coffee break.

It had been another pleasant day, winding down to a nice evening. Marti and Chris were snuggling in the porch glider Chris had made. The last meal of the day was over and put away. They were a good team with the cooking and tidying up, and now looked forward to talking over their day, the business, or some place they might like to go see someday. The muted ringing of their phone interrupted the quiet talking and they both made a fake frown as Marti left to answer it.

"That was Sena—following up on our talk of a girls' night out. It was so great seeing her again, but it was such a short visit we agreed to meet when there was more time."

Happy, easy-going Sena was good for Marti. Chris was happy for Marti as she looked forward to an evening in the company of the up-beat Sena.

It wasn't officially a "girls' night out." Sena had the day off and the two met for lunch at a new tearoom in the afternoon later in the week. The ambience was calming, noticeably quiet with soft lighting, attractive décor, and quite private. It would be exactly what Marti needed, time with a caring friend.

Sena had arrived first and picked out the most secluded area she saw and made herself comfortable while she waited.

Several minutes passed before a cheerful waitress popped her head in with Marti close behind, and pointing in Sena's direction announced, "There she is!"

As Marti neared the table, Sena stood and gave her a welcoming hug.

"At last, we can have some wonderful uninterrupted chat time just the two of us. Hope you're in no rush, Marti!" and Sena's special chuckle bubbled out.

There was a goodness in Sena that drew people to her and put them at ease. And for Marti there was also a sureness that there was nothing she could not trust to share with her friend. And she did want to share her troubling thoughts with this special woman.

Glasses of Zinfandel were poured; the waitress took their orders and the two friends grinned at each other in delighted anticipation and launched into catching Marti up on all matters in Decorah society that had occurred while she was in Red Wing. Marti told Sena of "Mincemeat" and his odd life and they laughed over him. Sena followed up with Narci's character flaws and the laughter flowed.

The food was delicious, and the friends' wine glasses had been refilled as the plates were cleared away. Sena, fingers toying with her wine glass, looked as though she were about to laugh again, but had leaned forward conspiratorially and whispered, "I'm seeing someone--seriously. His name's Curt."

Marti put a hand over her mouth to keep the laugh in. "Ah! Yes. Mr. Truman," and then did laugh at the surprise on Sena's face.

"You know him? You've met? How---??"

"Do you really want to know, Sena? Really?" So, Marti wiped her eyes and revealed the tale of the two black socks: one in Lillian's wastebasket and one in Sena's sheets. It was Sena's turn to wipe her eyes.

Gradually, a seriousness settled over the conversation and the perceptive Sena asked Marti what was troubling her because she knew something was, and it had nothing to do with Chris. The silence lasted while Marti, looking inward, searched for words to express her fears. Fear that her life that is so good again would disintegrate. What was wrong with her to think like that? She felt lost, at loose ends, with no purpose for her existence. And she asked again, expecting no answer, "What's wrong with me?"

Sena, in a low voice began to talk to Marti, with knowledge and understanding of the damage inflicted on women by abusive men. Marti listened, astonished, and then Sena paused saying softly, "I do know what you went through, Marti. I do not 'imagine' what you went through. I know."

Then, as if deciding something, Sena had unbuttoned a top button, folding back a bit of her blouse, and Marti saw old scars near the center of her chest. Then the blouse was back and buttoned again.

But it was at this point Sena brought the mood up a notch in the conversation. She told Marti of the abuse shelters where she had spoken. And of the meetings asking hard questions and listening to painful answers from women at the shelters. She encouraged Marti to put on paper all the things she wished she had done. And also name everyone who had helped her along her journey. To list all the things in retrospect she could have done--that might have helped her situation. What would she recommend to someone going through some of the things she had?

She asked Marti to go with her to a meeting soon--perhaps in time to share with others. It would help Marti begin to heal, as well as help others heal. There was so much need to let the light in on a very dark and deadly crime. Because that is what it was. A crime against women, without laws with teeth to combat it.

There was a lot of hard work ahead, all uphill, and it would take many hands, hearts and minds uniting to do anything about this evil.

Chris knew something had changed in Marti that day. It seemed something had wakened in her, and he heard an eagerness in her voice to turn the bad things in her memory into something useful for others. She would go with Sena and learn how to help others. Marti had a mission.

THE BEGINNING

AFTERWORD

It looked like a little Eden. A small white country church in an oak tree filled, woodsy setting at the end of a gravel road with another gravel road passing in front of the church forming a "T" intersection.

The large, old manse was directly across the road from the old church; and a church-owned rental house sat on the south side of the church parking lot.

A noisy stream flowed beneath a small bridge to the north of the church, and everywhere were great old trees with birds and squirrels. Lush green growth, the natural bushes and wildflowers were everywhere. Overhead was blue sky with small white clouds drifting.

The minister's young children could be heard playing in a sandbox in the backyard where a young pony waited patiently, with its head over the fence watching the children. A cat wandered around the sandbox, eyeing the sand where the youngsters played.

Mail had just been delivered, and the minister's wife took her time walking out to see what had been left. What a lovely day to be out. Before reaching the mailbox, she became aware of someone coming from between the two sheltering evergreens framing the cement walk to the front door of the rental house. She had heard there were new renters with young children there now. Collecting her mail from the box, she heard the approaching woman greet her and turned to respond in kind and found herself staring at a young mother who not only appeared half-starved but had an eye blackened and swollen closed.

She was so small, and so bony. Her hair unkempt, stringy, her clothes hung on her. When she introduced herself, there were gaps in her teeth. Three children huddled around her; the youngest, a toddler, never released her grip on the mother's skirt. A shaggy-haired, untidy boy, maybe six years old watched from behind his mother, and a bedraggled girl of perhaps eight, with long greasy hair looked anxiously from her mother's face to the neighbor's face and back again. Mute, expressionless children.

The shock for the minister's wife was such that she couldn't process what was being said and she could never recall by what name the woman introduced herself. But she clearly heard her ask, "Can my children play with your children?"

And the minister's wife had answered, "Of course! The youngest are in the sandbox, right back there." And she pointed towards the backyard and the two older children, silent, unsmiling, walked stiffly towards the play area. The toddler still clutched her mother's skirt.

A conversation, of sorts, was carried on and the minister's wife had finally asked how the black eye had happened, and when she learned--to her everlasting shame--never told anyone. That's the way it was fifty years ago.

But she never forgot the wreck of a young woman's sad voice saying, "My husband hits me. I know he's always sorry, though. He tells me he won't do it again. He always tells me he loves me afterwards. He always says he loves me."

It was later learned that as the two mothers talked that day, the shaggy-haired, ragtag six-year-old boy had "tackled" the minister's six-year-old, youngest girl, knocking her to the ground and climbing on top of her, began kissing her. Apples don't fall far from the tree—a brute of a father had already "trained up a son" like himself.

That night as the minister, his wife and six children slept peacefully in their beds, in the perfect silence of the country—except for crickets and the occasional "who-whoing" of owls. The night was cool, moonlit, all the windows open to a soft breeze.

But mothers are light sleepers, and the minister's wife woke suddenly, sitting straight up in bed, then quickly was across the room and kneeling at an open window to the front yard, and "kitty-corner" to the neighbor's house, and she looked everywhere in the moonlit scene.

There was not a sound to be heard. No movement of any kind, just the flat stretch of road going south. No lights were, or could have been, seen through the trees at the rental house. But she had clearly heard a cry in the night, "Help me!"

On Sunday at church, the minister's wife made inquiries about the new family, with no one seeming to know anything about them until one of the men of the church overheard her asking, and said, "They packed up and moved out in the middle of the night."

And now, fifty-two years later, an elderly woman slyly smiles into her favorite cup, emblazoned with the statement— "Please do not annoy the writer, she may put you in a book and kill you." The writer never met the brute who left a ruined woman and three destroyed children in his wake, but she named him "Ted" and put him in her book, endowing him with everything: movie star good looks, intelligence, wealth, charm, and success with the ladies; and then--she killed him! Damn, that felt good!

Lightning Source UK Ltd.
Milton Keynes UK
UKHW010643300721
388036UK00002B/405